NO LONGER
THE SEATTLE PUBLIC

DEC 0 2
D0548876

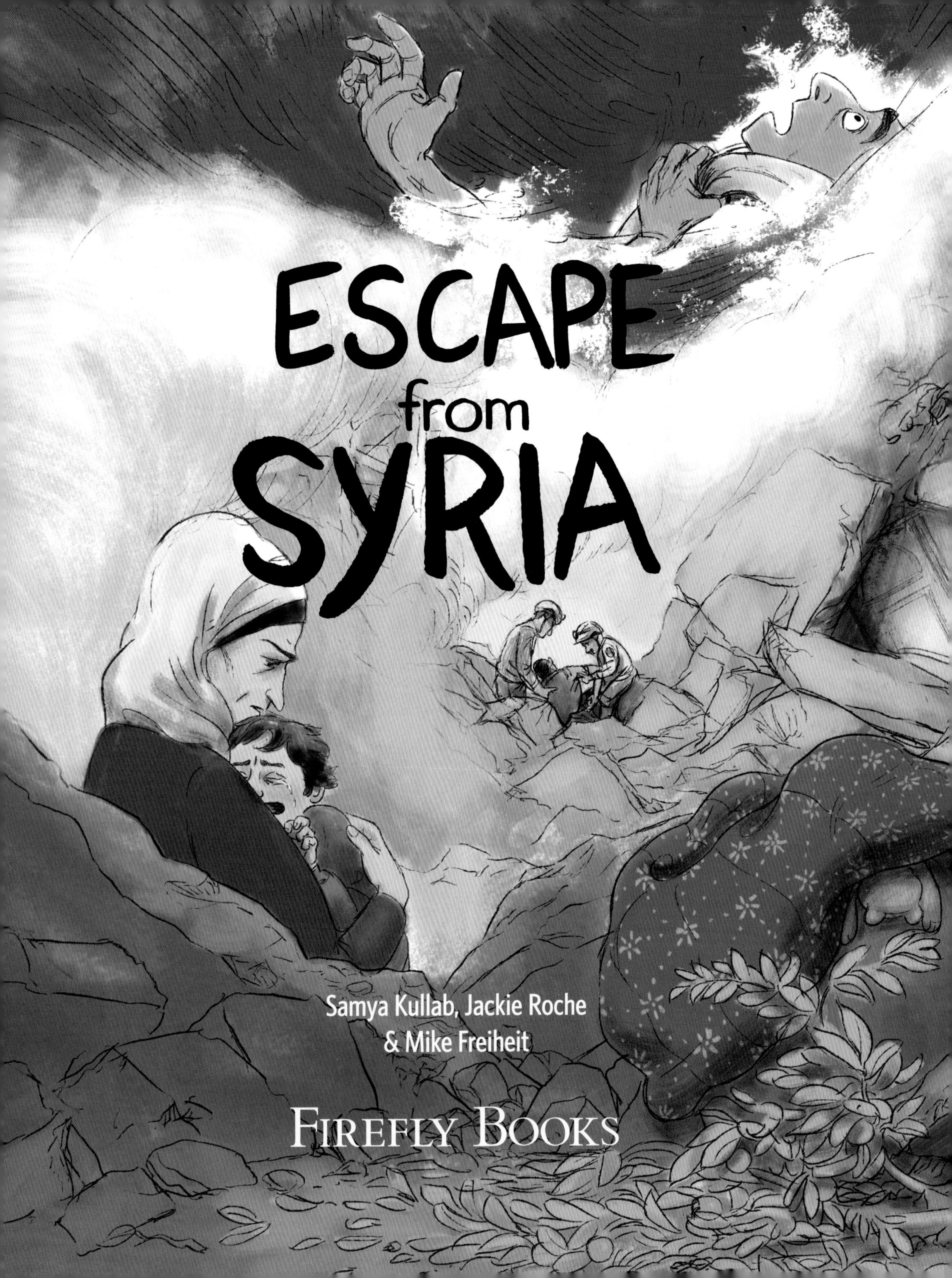

ESCAPE from SYRIA

Samya Kullab, Jackie Roche
& Mike Freiheit

FIREFLY BOOKS

A FIREFLY BOOK

Published by Firefly Books Ltd. 2017
Copyright © 2017 Firefly Books Ltd.
Text copyright © 2017 Samya Kullab
Illustrations copyright © 2017 Jackie Roche
Photos copyright © as listed on this page.

All rights reserved. No part of this publication may be reproduced, stored in a retrieval system, or transmitted in any form or by any means, electronic, mechanical, photocopying, recording or otherwise, without the prior written permission of the Publisher.

First printing

Publisher Cataloging-in-Publication Data (U.S.)

Names: Kullab, Samya, author. | Roche, Jackie, illustrator. | Freiheit, Mike, colorist.
Title: Escape From Syria / story by Samya Kullab ; illustrations by Jackie Roche ; colors by Mike Freiheit.
Description: Richmond Hill, Ontario, Canada : Firefly Books, 2017. | Summary: "A fictionalized account of a family fleeing war-torn Syria after their home in Aleppo is destroyed. They endure wretched refugee camps, ocean crossings and swindlers — all to find safety in the West" – Provided by publisher.
Identifiers: ISBN 978-1-77085-982-1 (hardcover)
Subjects: LCSH: Refugee families - Comic books, strips, etc. | Refugee camps—Lebanon - Comic books, strips, etc. | Syria—History—Civil War, 2011- — Comic books, strips, etc. | BISACSH: JUVENILE FICTION/ Comics & Graphic Novels / General. | JUVENILE FICTION/ People & Places / Middle East. | JUVENILE FICTION/ Social Themes / Emigration & Immigration.
Classification: LCC PZ7.7K855Es |DDC 741.5973 – dc23

Library and Archives Canada Cataloguing in Publication

A CIP record for this title is available from Library and Archives Canada

Published in the United States by
Firefly Books (U.S.) Inc.
P.O. Box 1338, Ellicott Station
Buffalo, New York 14205

Published in Canada by
Firefly Books Ltd.
50 Staples Avenue, Unit 1
Richmond Hill, Ontario L4B 0A7

Colorist: Mike Freiheit
Text design: Sam Tse
Printed in China

 We acknowledge the financial support of the Government of Canada.

Photo Credits

88 Reuters/Handout
89 Reuters/Bassam Khabieh
90 Reuters/Mohamed Azakir
91 L Reuters/Ali Hashisho
91 R, 93 L Reuters/Stringer

92 Reuters/Ammar Abdullah
93 R Reuters/Osman Orsal
93 B Reuters/Laszlo Balogh
94 Reuters/Sultan Kitaz

To my aunt, Shahruk Rahman, who told me to write.

— S.K.

To the generous and hard-working Syrian refugee families I have had the pleasure to meet in the Greater Chicago area. I am so glad that we are neighbors.

— J.R.

Introduction

As the civil war entered its third year in 2013, I started reporting on Syrian refugees for the English-language Lebanese newspaper, the *Daily Star*. By then, most new arrivals to Lebanon were concentrated just inside the country's borders. As the years went by, their presence swelled from a few thousand to well over one million — about one-fifth of Lebanon's population. Much of my reporting documented the deteriorating circumstances of refugees, from difficult to intolerable.

It didn't take long before makeshift camps began to dot Lebanon's rural landscape. Those camps — now home to hundreds of thousands — are a testament to the harsh domestic policies Lebanese lawmakers instituted to ensure refugees could not integrate into Lebanese society.

With the constant influx of people, Lebanese infrastructure and social resources were taxed beyond their limits. Hospital waiting rooms were beset by long lineups of Syrians seeking medical assistance. Garbage piled up on streets, jobs for refugees were scarce and the majority of the population spiraled into crippling debt. In 2013, the United Nations High Commissioner for Refugees (UNHCR) estimated that 200,000 Syrian children would likely go without formal schooling because Lebanon's education ministry was unable to accommodate them. That same year, the World Bank reported that the Syrian conflict had cost Lebanon $7.5 billion in economic losses.

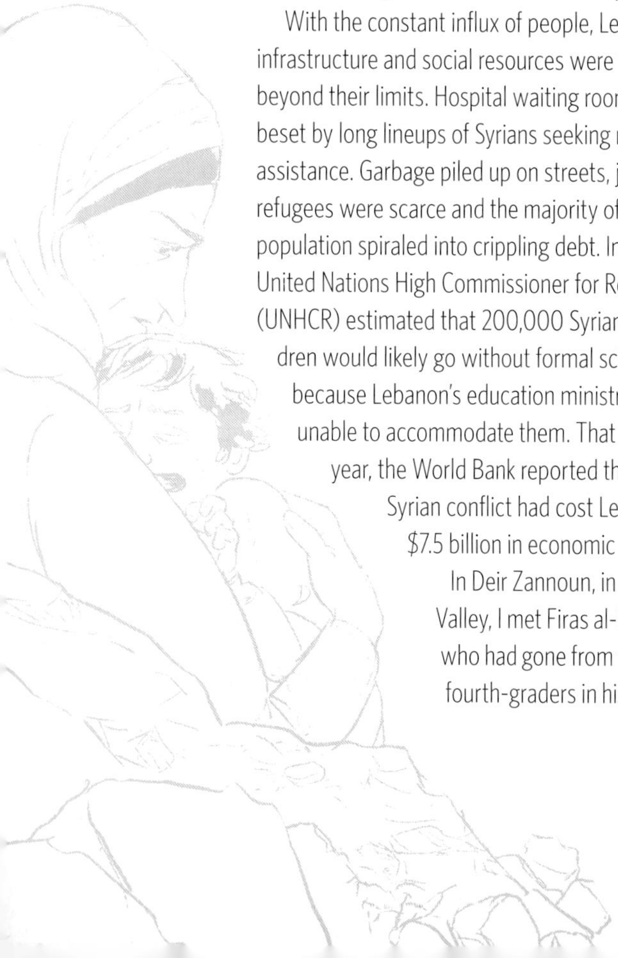

In Deir Zannoun, in the Bekaa Valley, I met Firas al-Homsi, who had gone from teaching fourth-graders in his native Hama, Syria, to knocking door to door at the elementary schools of Bar Elias to see if any could take his 8-year-old son, Mahmoud. "Without education, we have no future," he had said then, sitting on a straw mat in what he thought would be a temporary home. Four years on, Firas is still in Lebanon, and Mahmoud, now 12, has still not gone to school. That same trip, I met Nadim, a 7-year-old who began his days at 5 a.m. working as a blacksmith's assistant and ended them dashing down a sunset-tinged hill to his camp with soot-covered hands.

In *Escape From Syria*, Amina is a fictional protagonist, but her story is inspired by the strength and determination of the Syrian youth I've encountered who have had no choice but to grow up fast in the midst of hostility and hardship. The grim reality of Amina's life in Lebanon is the same one that thousands of young Syrians have involuntarily met. The fates of the real-life Aminas are reflected in the shocking statistics periodically issued by UN agencies: Approximately half of school-aged Syrian children in Lebanon are out of school; an ever-increasing number of Syrian children are being exploited in the labor market (including children as young as 6 in Lebanon); nearly 90 percent of Syrian

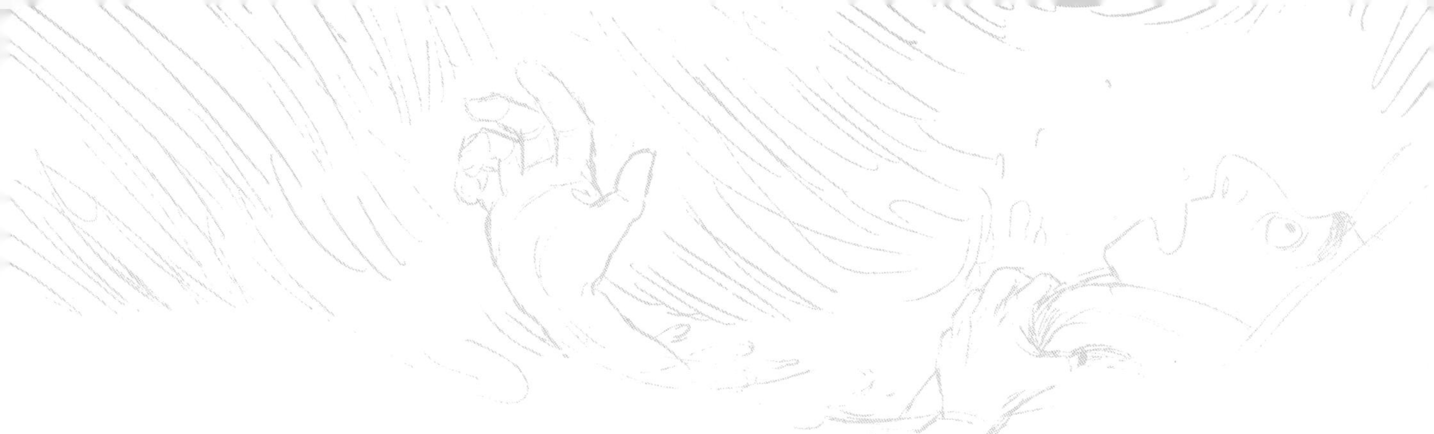

refugees in Lebanon are trapped in debt; and without a means to provide for their families, a rising number of Syrian parents are arranging marriages for their children, sometimes for those as young as 9. According to one report on arranged marriages, as many as 23 percent of female Syrian refugees have become child brides.

Amina's parents, Walid and Dalia, face the same extremely difficult choices real Syrian parents must make every day to survive as refugee families in Lebanon. In late 2015, a new Lebanese law requiring Syrians to relinquish their refugee status if they sought employment made an already untenable situation dire for many families. In Bisserieh, southern Lebanon, several parents told me that they were coping by eating one meal a day and rarely consuming meat. Many had accumulated large debts with shop owners, pharmacists and neighbors. Mustafa Halabi, a refugee in Sidon, said he reduced his daily food intake so his children wouldn't starve.

As the war entered its fifth year in 2015, some of the refugees I had met were desperate enough to risk their lives to cross the Aegean Sea to Europe. Dozens died as boats capsized en route to the Turkish coast from Tripoli, in northern Lebanon. But some, like Mohamed al-Zohouri, a Syrian refugee from Homs, boasted proudly on social media that he had made it. His story — he eventually settled in Sweden — and others like it provide a glimmer of hope to those languishing in refugee camps.

Resettlement, however, has always been limited to a lucky few, and even those selected must face the long, difficult work of integration. In 2016, I followed several Syrian families who had been resettled in Canada as part of a special program initiated by the ruling Liberal government. The majority of refugees accepted for Canadian resettlement were large families with young children; others identified as LGBTQ and had faced persecution in Middle East host countries, while others had fled Syria for political reasons.

I was surprised by how many parents said they were at first unwilling to leave the Middle East because they hoped to return to Syria one day. In the end, many said they chose resettlement to give their children a better life, and most hoped to have their extended family members who continued to live under fire in Syria join them one day.

Long after leaving Lebanon in December 2015, I still get messages from Syrian refugees. They report of deteriorating conditions in the camps, daily struggles and worsening health; they ask for help contacting Western embassies. While diplomats float the idea of creating safe zones in Syria, refugees say they would not feel safe returning home with Bashar al-Assad at the helm of the country. For now, they remain stuck in an interminable limbo. "It's like living in a nightmare," Matar Ibrahim, a refugee in Zahle, Lebanon, told me once when I asked him about the future. "But life still goes on."

I hope the story of Amina and her family educates and inspires readers, but mostly, I hope it humanizes this real-life nightmare.

— Samya Kullab, June 2017

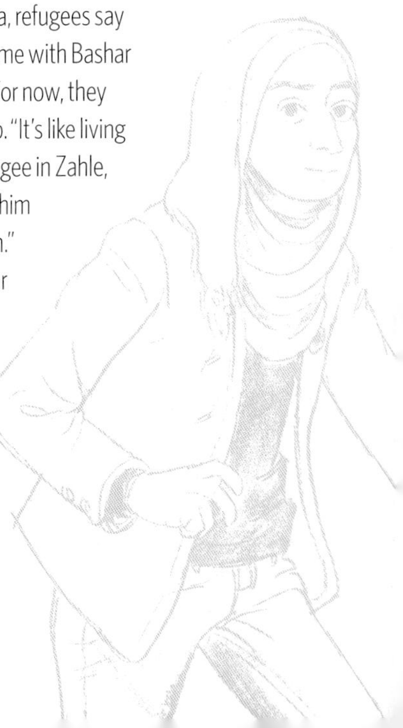

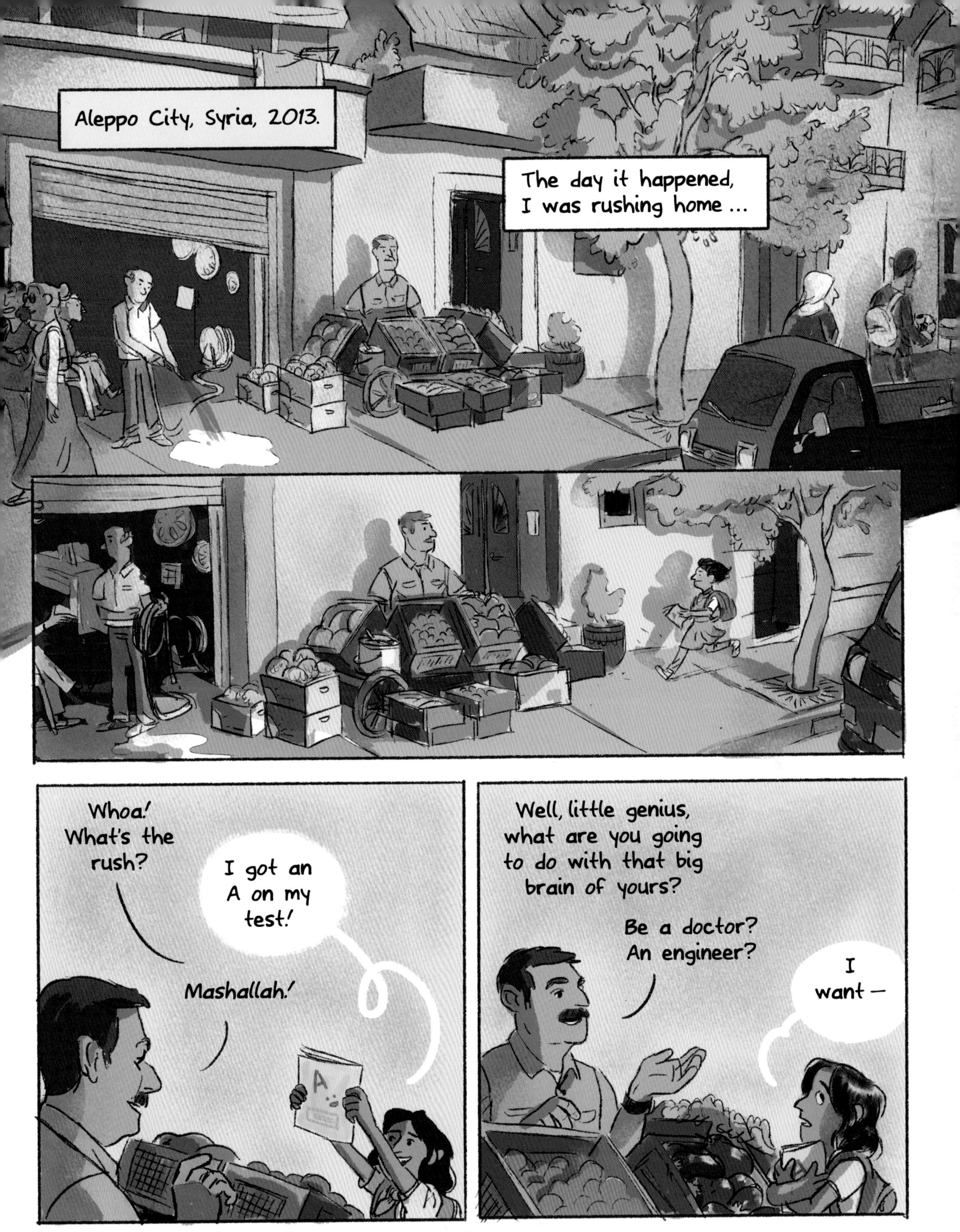
Aleppo City, Syria, 2013.
The day it happened, I was rushing home ...
Whoa! What's the rush?
I got an A on my test!
Mashallah!
Well, little genius, what are you going to do with that big brain of yours?
Be a doctor? An engineer?
I want —

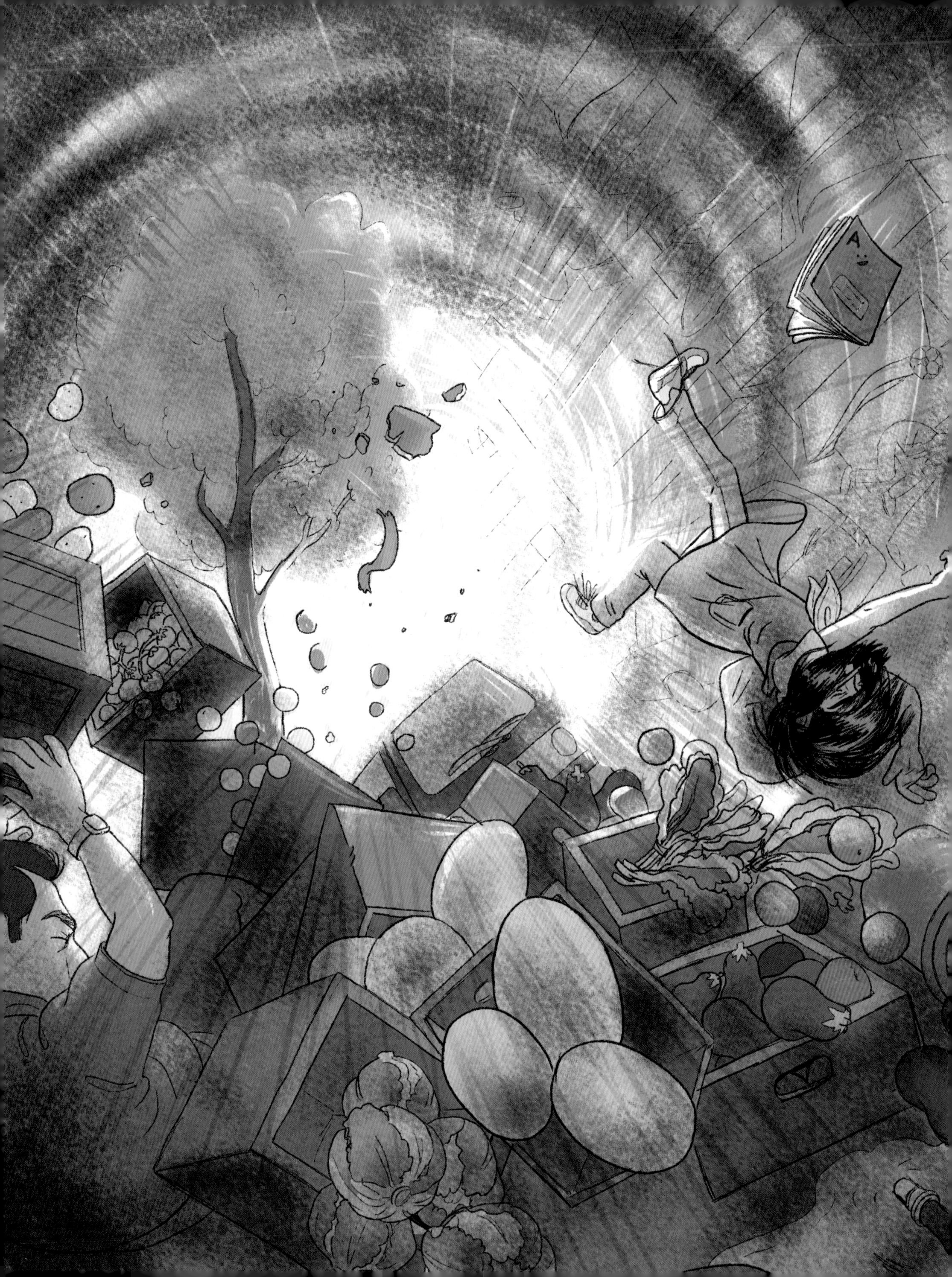

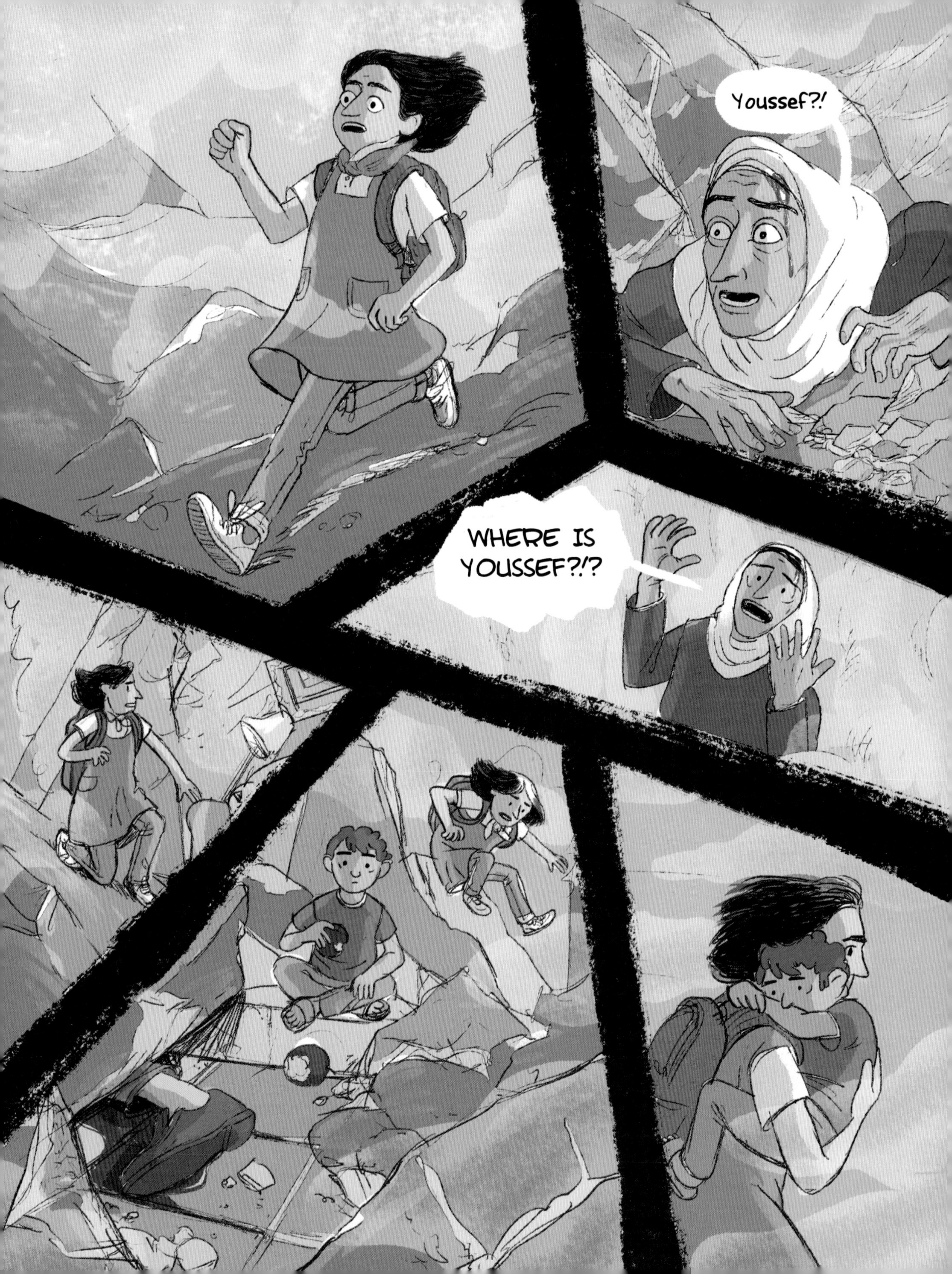
Youssef?!
WHERE IS YOUSSEF?!?

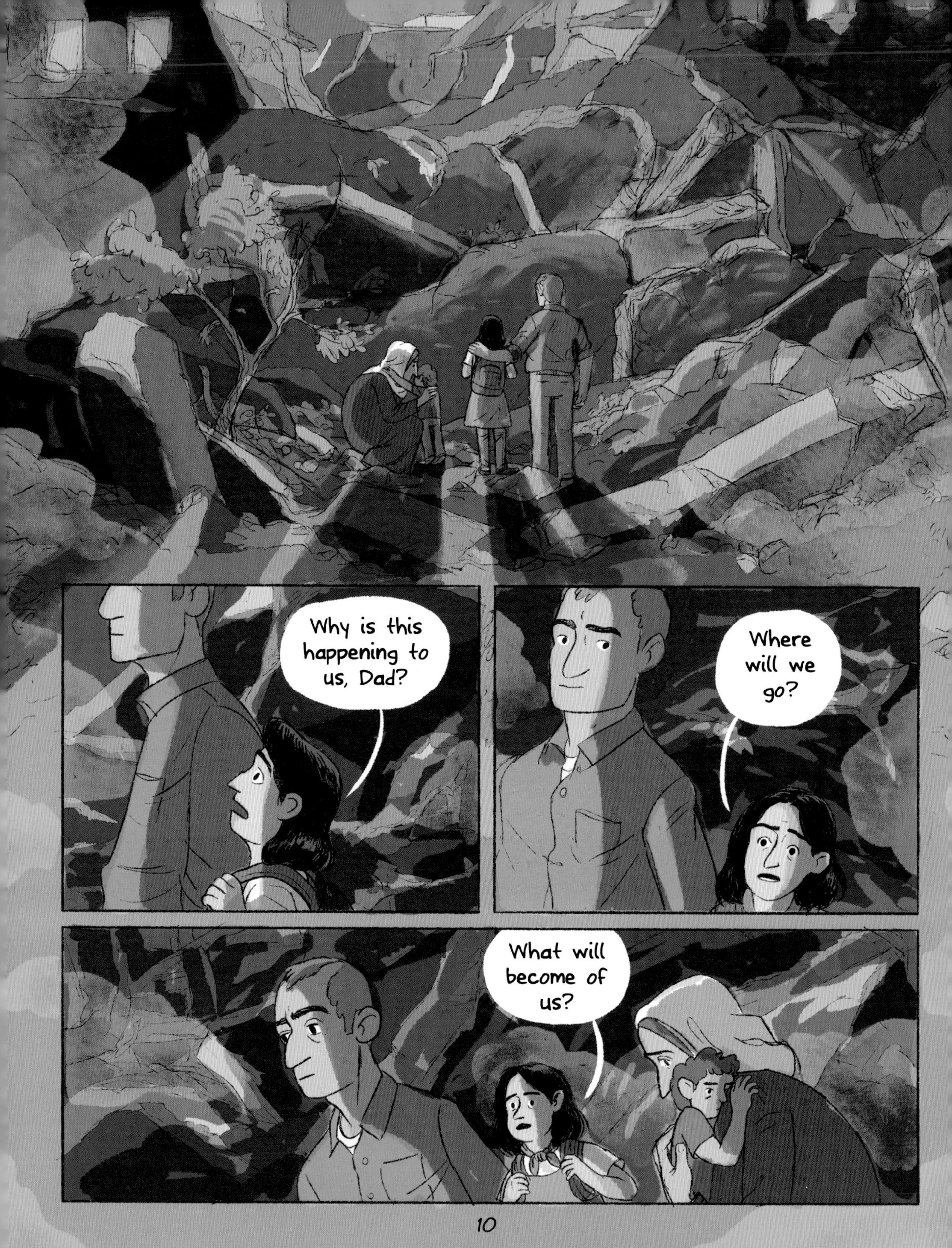
Why is this happening to us, Dad?
Where will we go?
What will become of us?

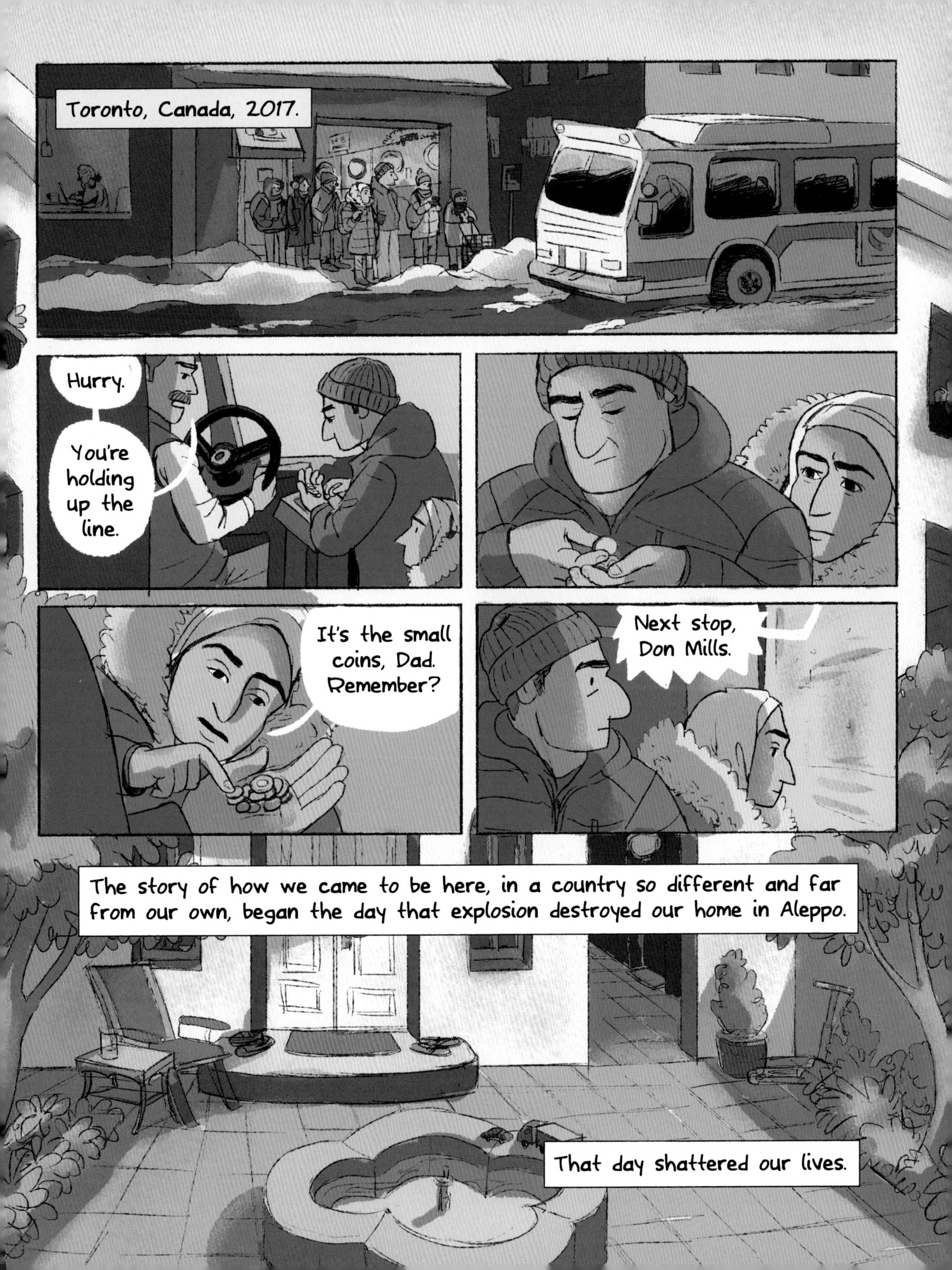
Toronto, Canada, 2017.
Hurry.
You're holding up the line.
It's the small coins, Dad. Remember?
Next stop, Don Mills.
The story of how we came to be here, in a country so different and far from our own, began the day that explosion destroyed our home in Aleppo.
That day shattered our lives.

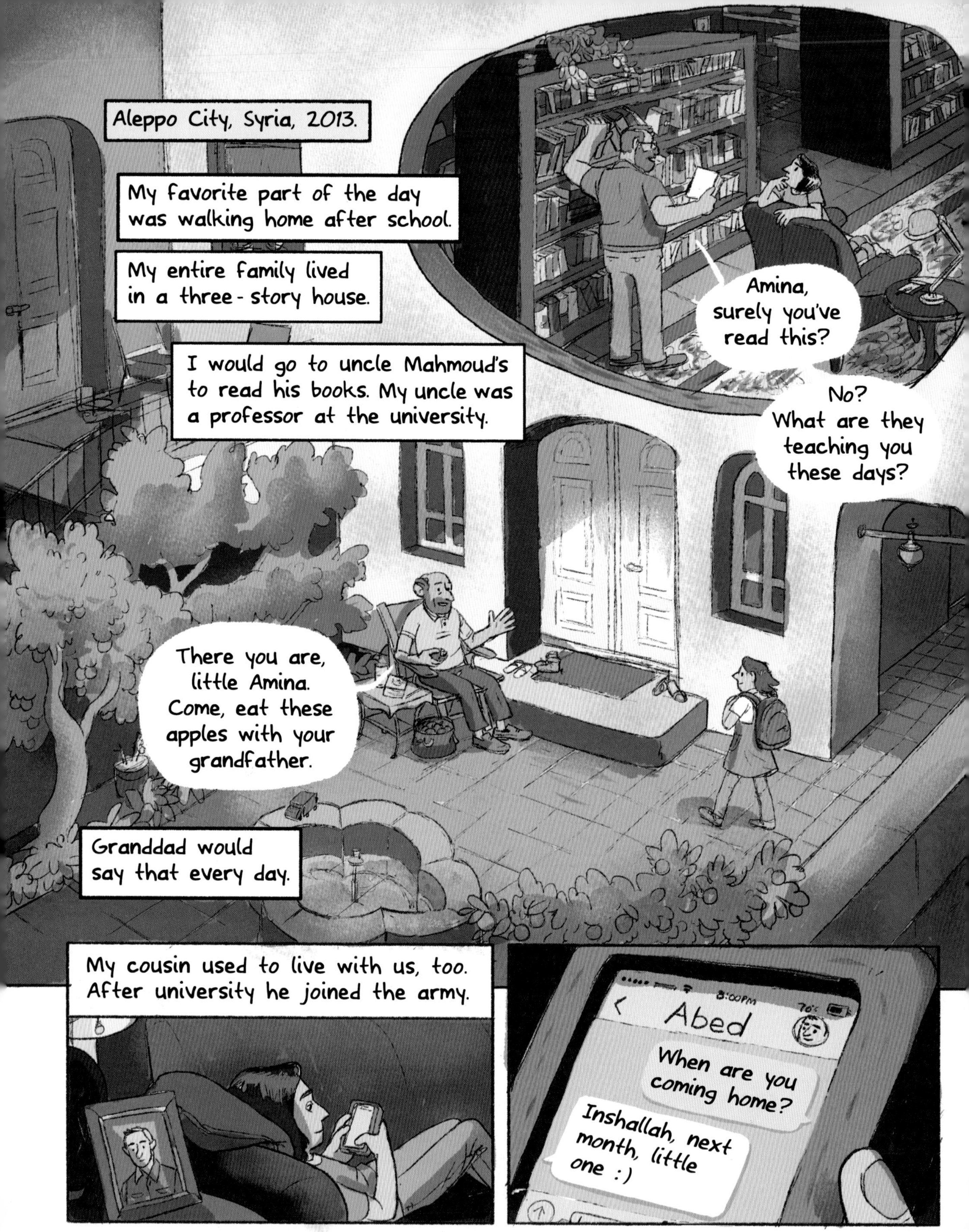
Aleppo City, Syria, 2013.
My favorite part of the day was walking home after school.
My entire family lived in a three-story house.
I would go to uncle Mahmoud's to read his books. My uncle was a professor at the university.
Amina, surely you've read this?
No? What are they teaching you these days?
There you are, little Amina. Come, eat these apples with your grandfather.
Granddad would say that every day.
My cousin used to live with us, too. After university he joined the army.
8:00PM
Abed
When are you coming home?
Inshallah, next month, little one :)

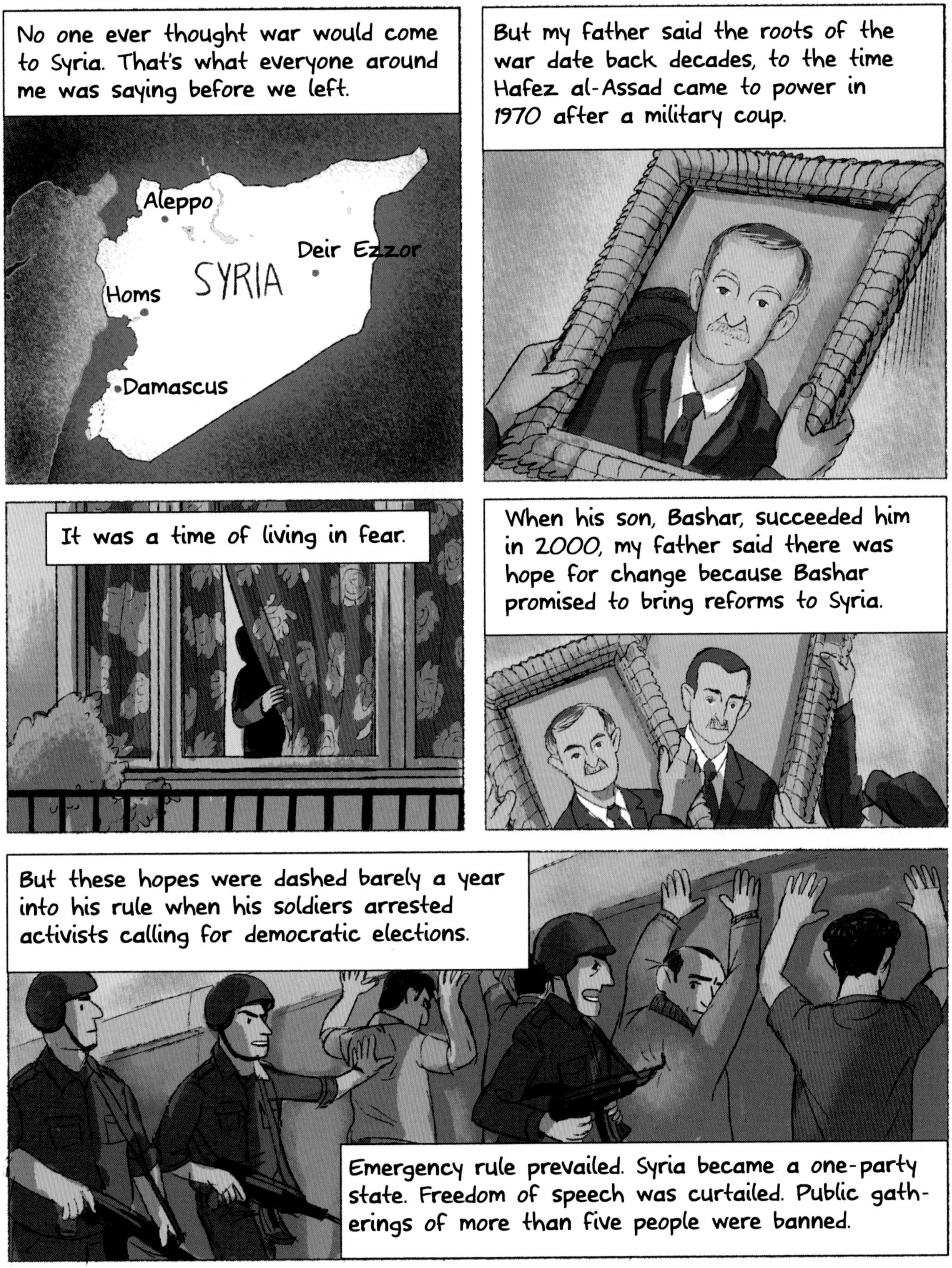
No one ever thought war would come to Syria. That's what everyone around me was saying before we left.
Aleppo
Deir Ezzor
SYRIA
Homs
Damascus
But my father said the roots of the war date back decades, to the time Hafez al-Assad came to power in 1970 after a military coup.
It was a time of living in fear.
When his son, Bashar, succeeded him in 2000, my father said there was hope for change because Bashar promised to bring reforms to Syria.
But these hopes were dashed barely a year into his rule when his soldiers arrested activists calling for democratic elections.
Emergency rule prevailed. Syria became a one-party state. Freedom of speech was curtailed. Public gath-erings of more than five people were banned.

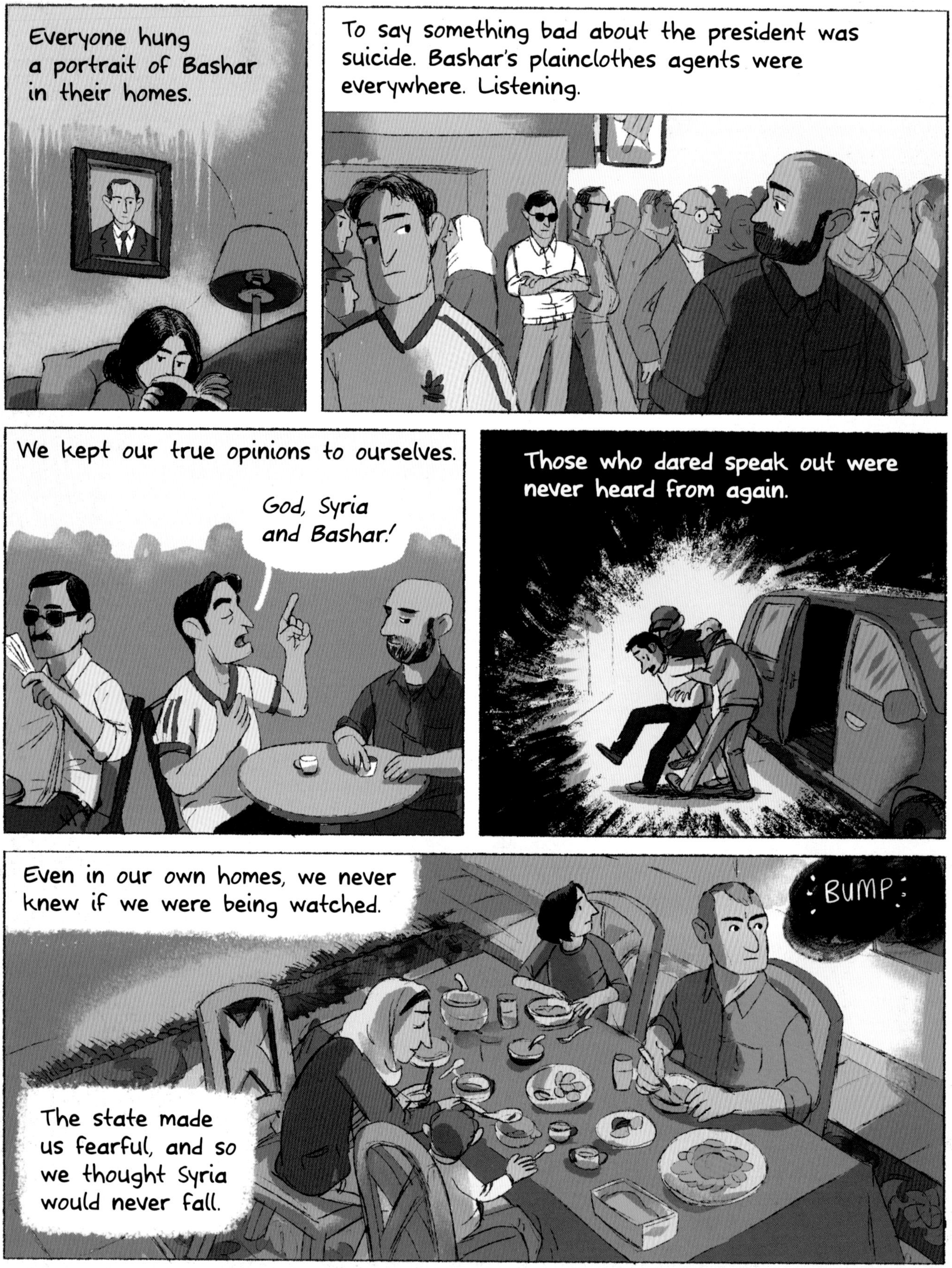
Everyone hung a portrait of Bashar in their homes.
To say something bad about the president was suicide. Bashar's plainclothes agents were everywhere. Listening.
We kept our true opinions to ourselves.
God, Syria and Bashar!
Those who dared speak out were never heard from again.
Even in our own homes, we never knew if we were being watched.
BUMP
The state made us fearful, and so we thought Syria would never fall.

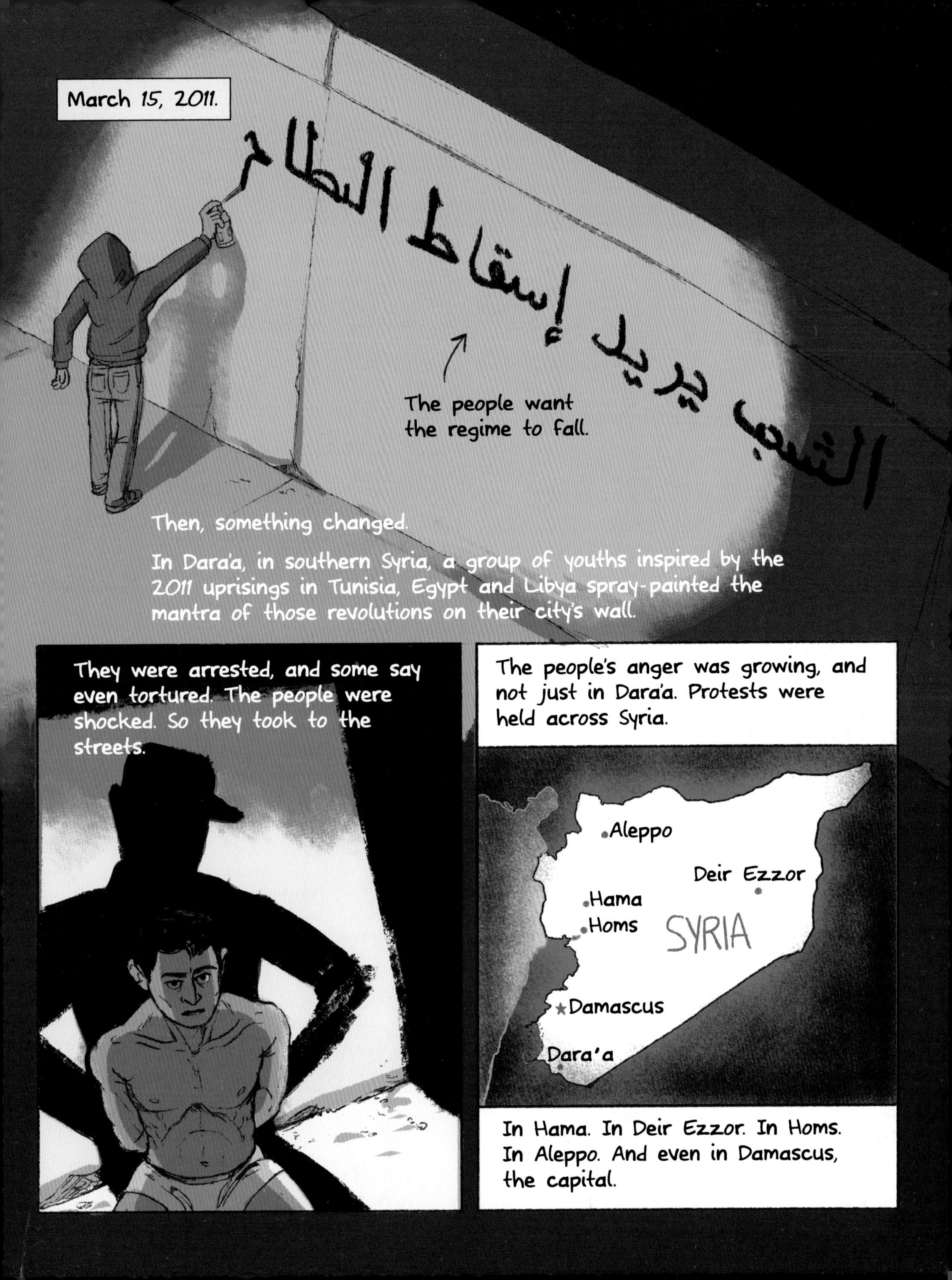
March 15, 2011.
الشعب يريد إسقاط النظام
The people want the regime to fall.
Then, something changed.
In Dara'a, in southern Syria, a group of youths inspired by the 2011 uprisings in Tunisia, Egypt and Libya spray-painted the mantra of those revolutions on their city's wall.
They were arrested, and some say even tortured. The people were shocked. So they took to the streets.
The people's anger was growing, and not just in Dara'a. Protests were held across Syria.
Aleppo
Deir Ezzor
Hama
Homs
SYRIA
Damascus
Dara'a
In Hama. In Deir Ezzor. In Homs. In Aleppo. And even in Damascus, the capital.

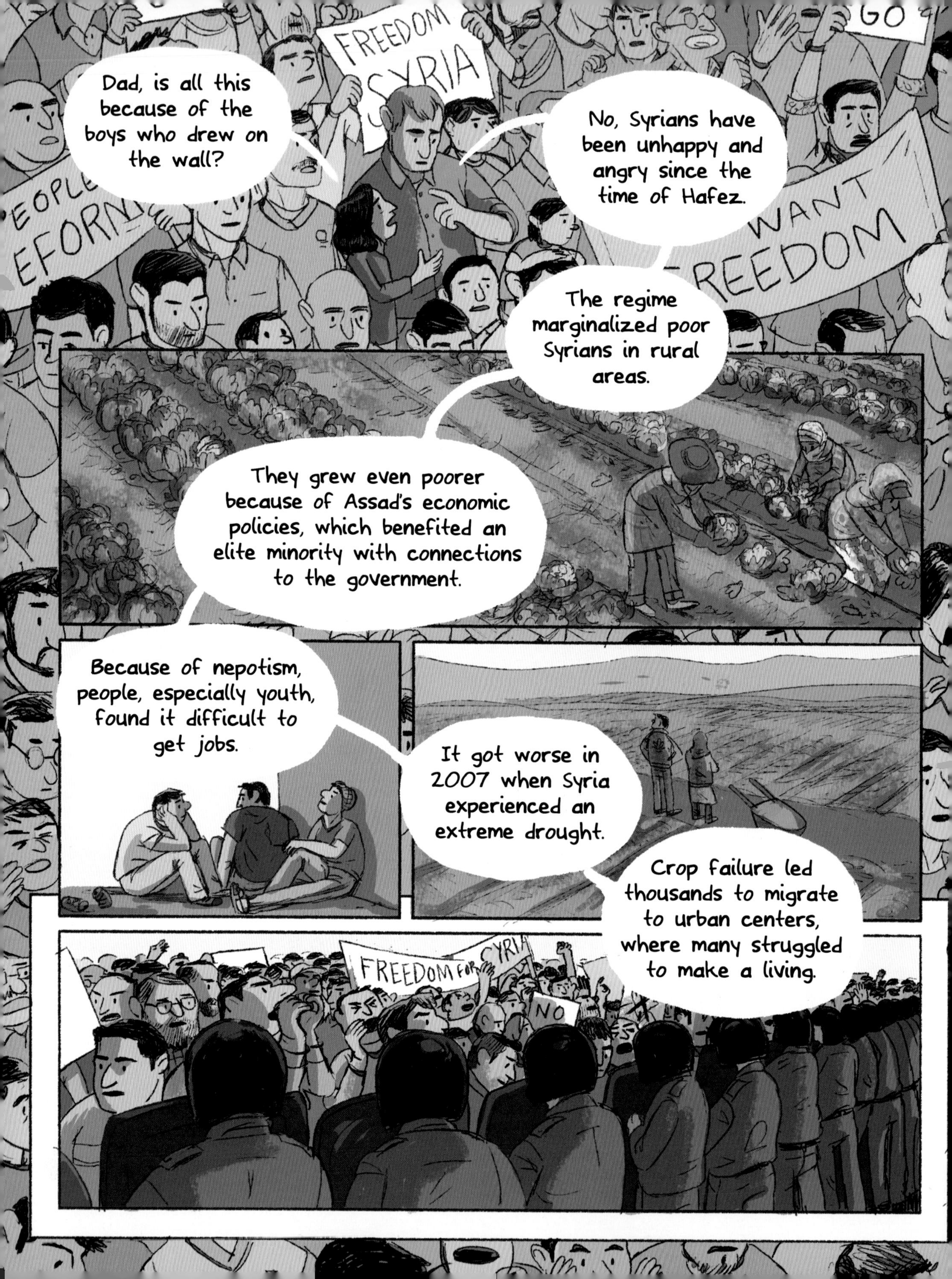
FREEDOM
SYRIA
GO
Dad, is all this because of the boys who drew on the wall?
No, Syrians have been unhappy and angry since the time of Hafez.
EOPLE
EFORM
WANT
FREEDOM
The regime marginalized poor Syrians in rural areas.
They grew even poorer because of Assad's economic policies, which benefited an elite minority with connections to the government.
Because of nepotism, people, especially youth, found it difficult to get jobs.
It got worse in 2007 when Syria experienced an extreme drought.
Crop failure led thousands to migrate to urban centers, where many struggled to make a living.
FREEDOM FOR SYRIA
NO

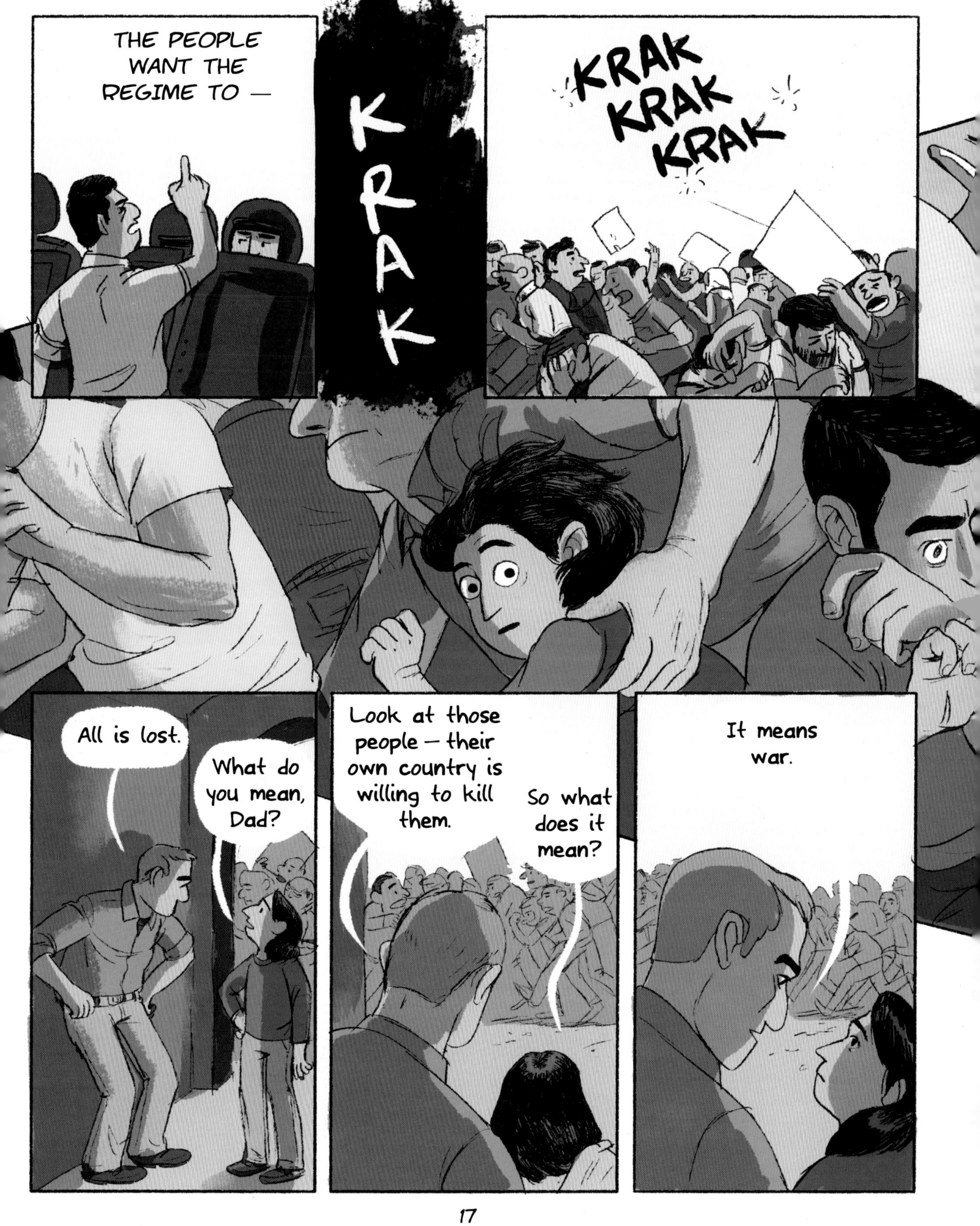
THE PEOPLE WANT THE REGIME TO —
KRAK
KRAK KRAK KRAK
All is lost.
What do you mean, Dad?
Look at those people — their own country is willing to kill them.
So what does it mean?
It means war.

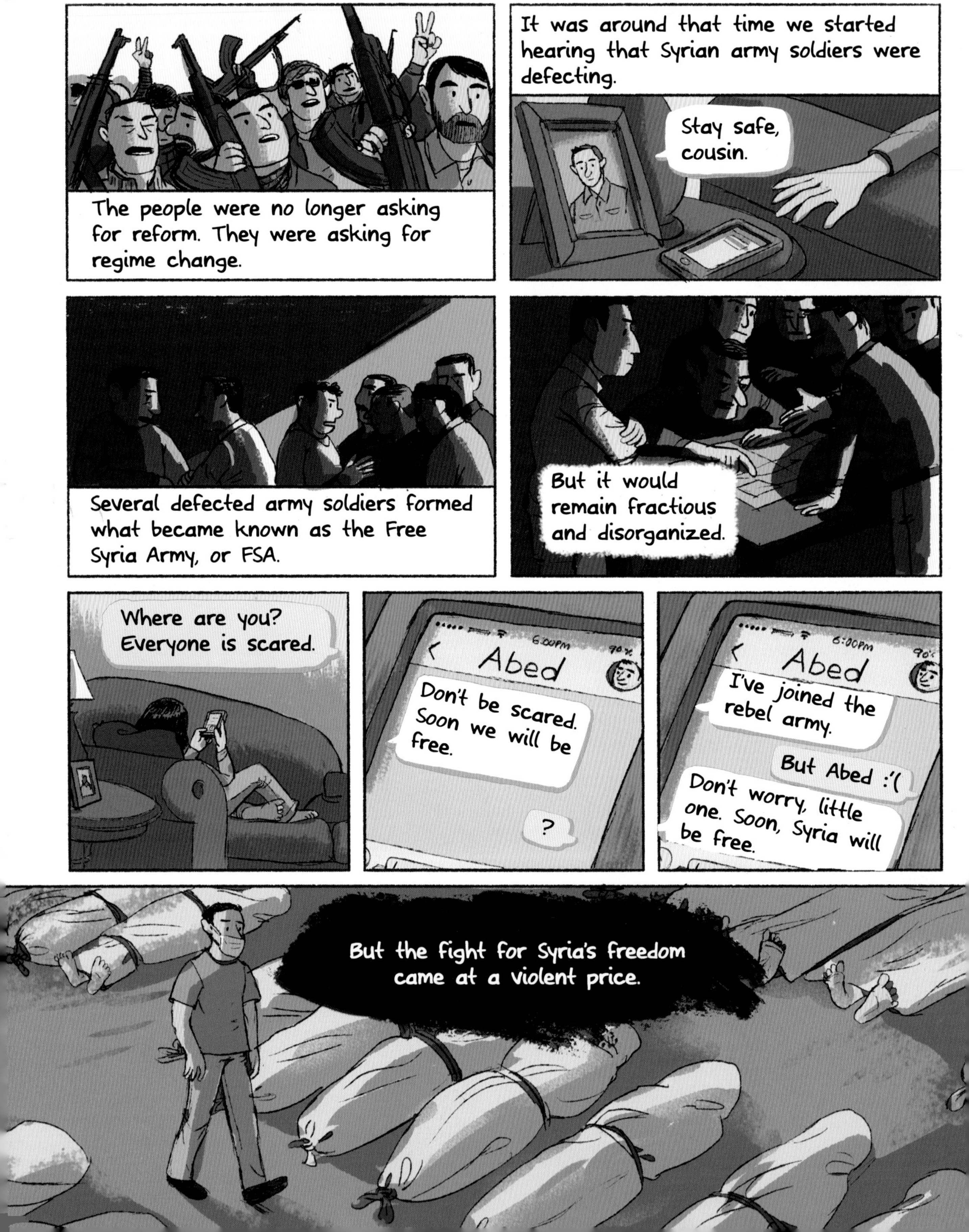
The people were no longer asking for reform. They were asking for regime change.
It was around that time we started hearing that Syrian army soldiers were defecting.
Stay safe, cousin.
Several defected army soldiers formed what became known as the Free Syria Army, or FSA.
But it would remain fractious and disorganized.
Where are you? Everyone is scared.
Abed
Don't be scared. Soon we will be free.
?
Abed
I've joined the rebel army.
But Abed :'(
Don't worry, little one. Soon, Syria will be free.
But the fight for Syria's freedom came at a violent price.

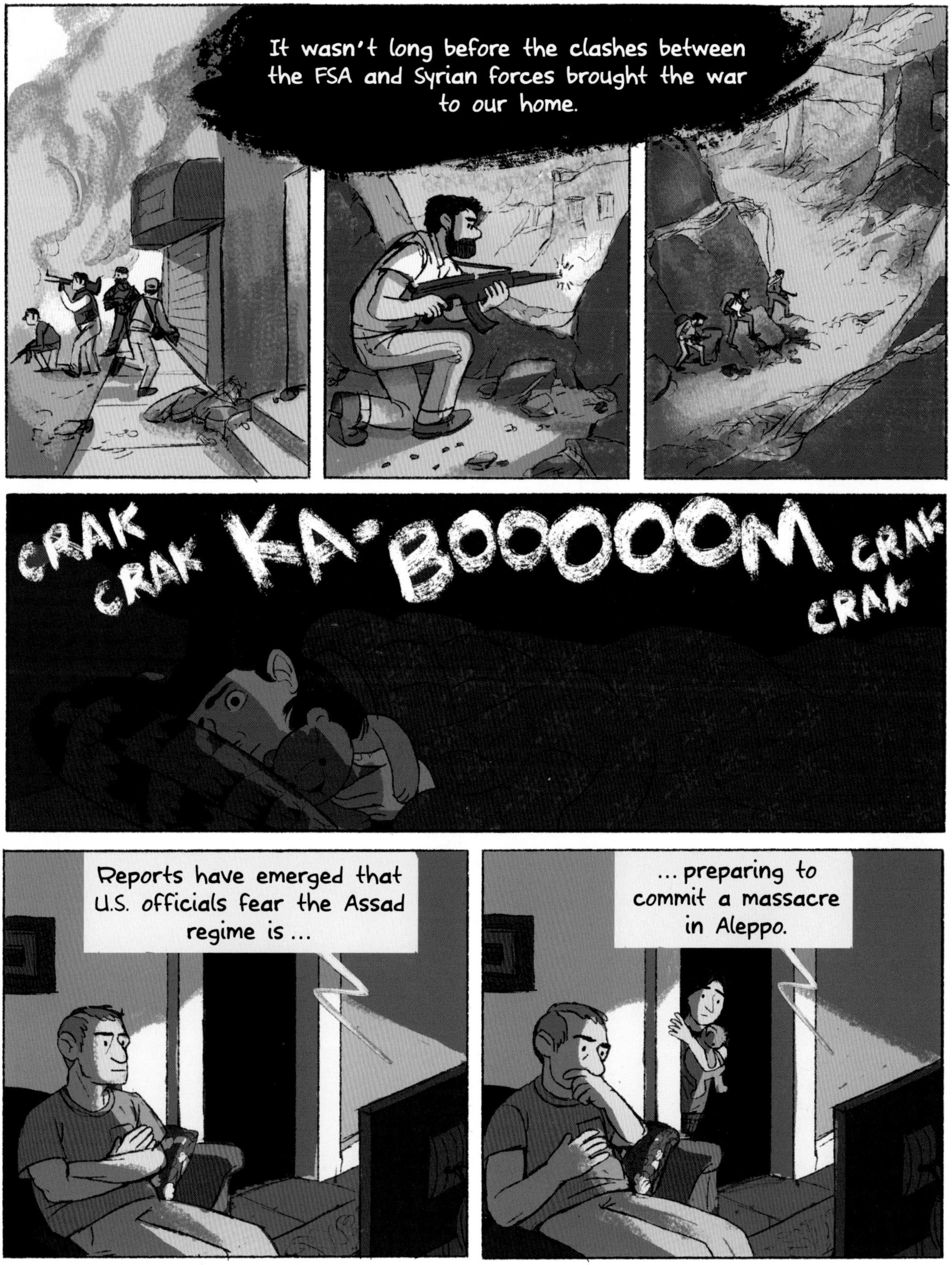

It wasn't long before the clashes between the FSA and Syrian forces brought the war to our home.
CRAK CRAK KA-BOOOOOM CRAK CRAK
Reports have emerged that U.S. officials fear the Assad regime is ...
... preparing to commit a massacre in Aleppo.

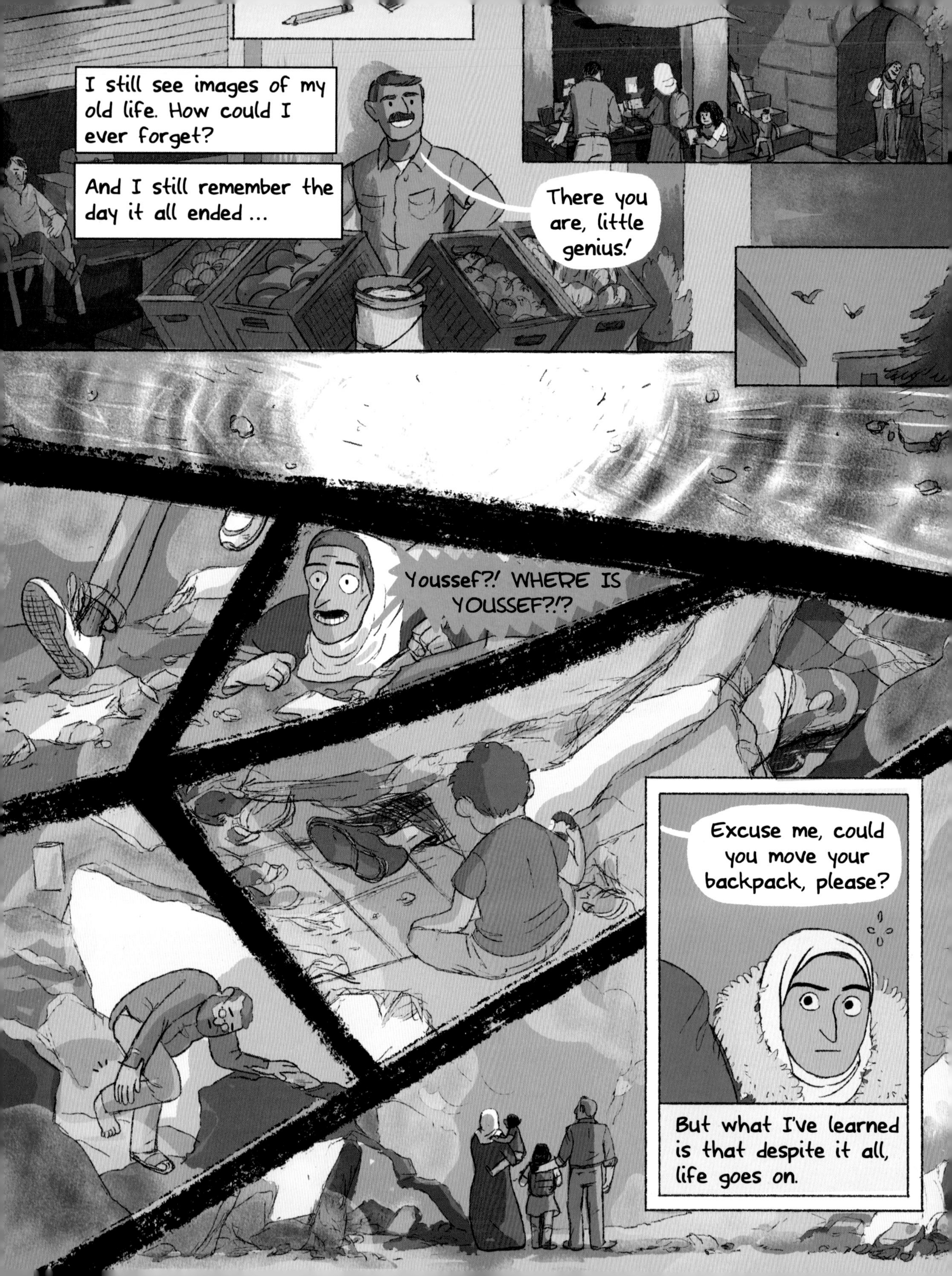
I still see images of my old life. How could I ever forget?
And I still remember the day it all ended ...
There you are, little genius!
Youssef?! WHERE IS YOUSSEF?!?
Excuse me, could you move your backpack, please?
But what I've learned is that despite it all, life goes on.

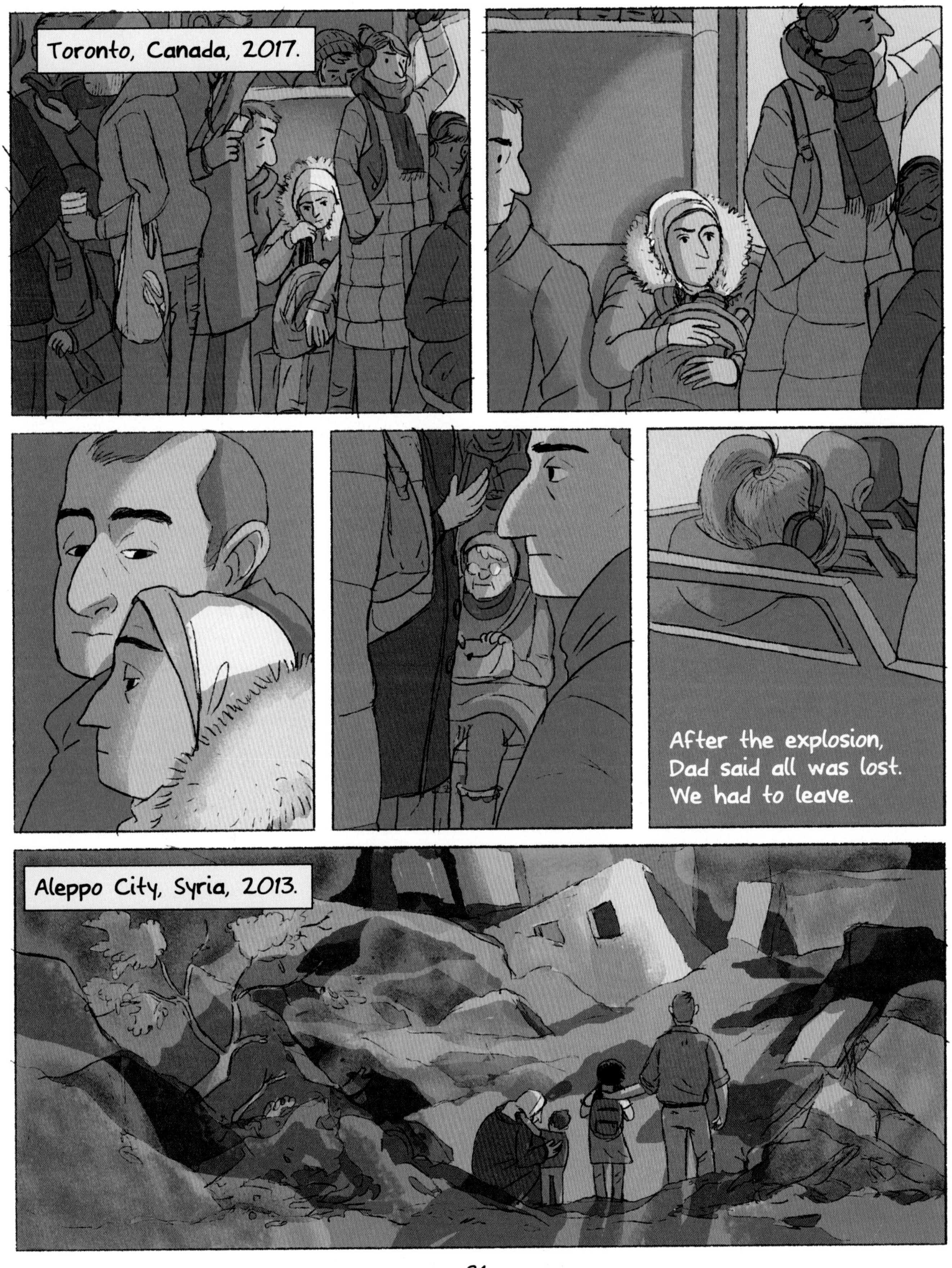
Toronto, Canada, 2017.
After the explosion, Dad said all was lost. We had to leave.
Aleppo City, Syria, 2013.

It will only be for a little while.

وعندما أرطل برأُحدو
اني يتدنت كل مابوجتي لابقى

↑

When I leave,
be sure I tried
everything in my
power to stay.

Lebanon-Syria border, 2013.

Let us through!

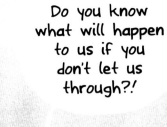

Do you know what will happen to us if you don't let us through?!

STAMP

Only six months? Do you think the war will end so soon?

مرحبا بكم في لبنان
Welcome to Lebanon

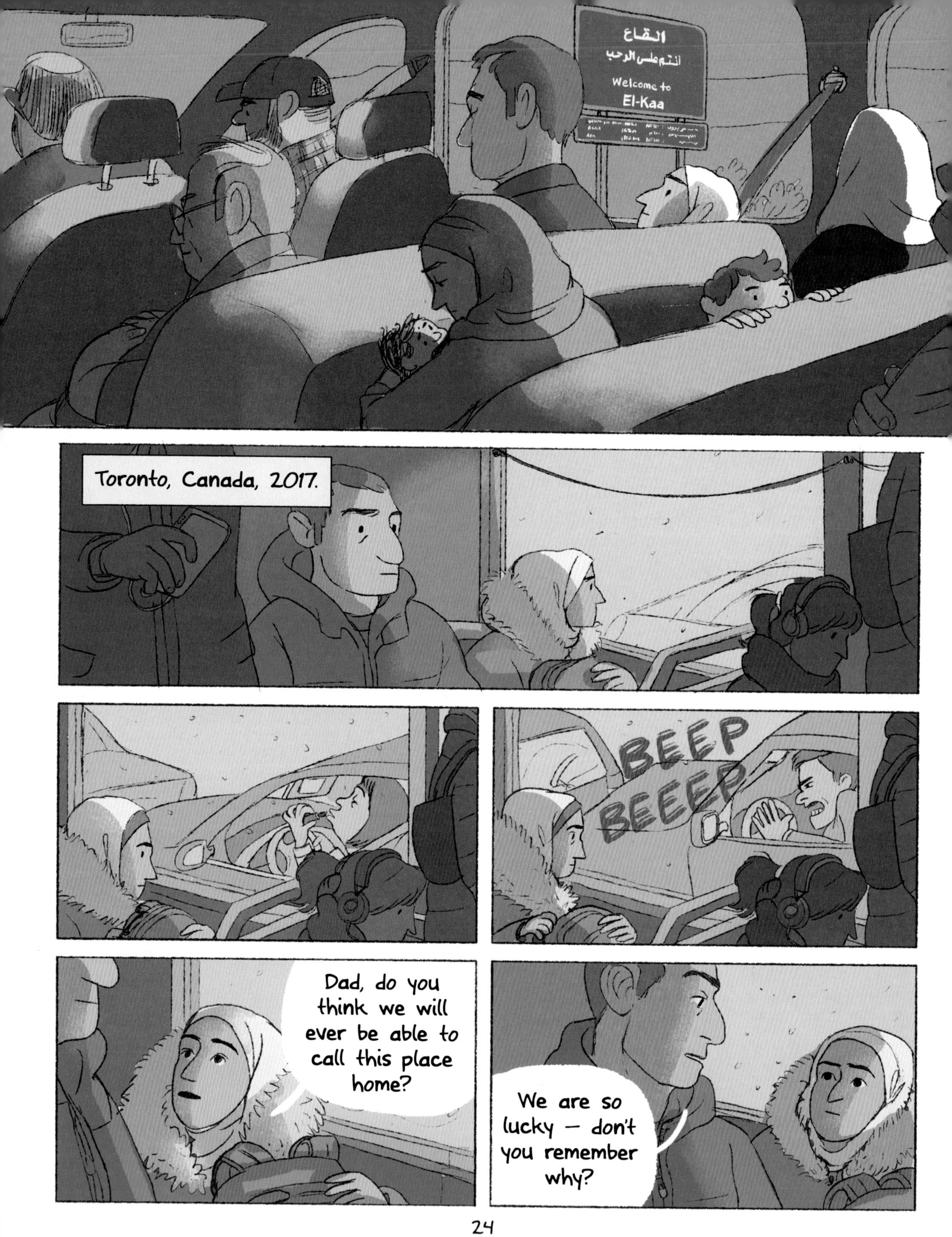
القاع
انتم على الرحب
Welcome to
El-Kaa
Toronto, Canada, 2017.
BEEP
BEEEP
Dad, do you think we will ever be able to call this place home?
We are so lucky — don't you remember why?

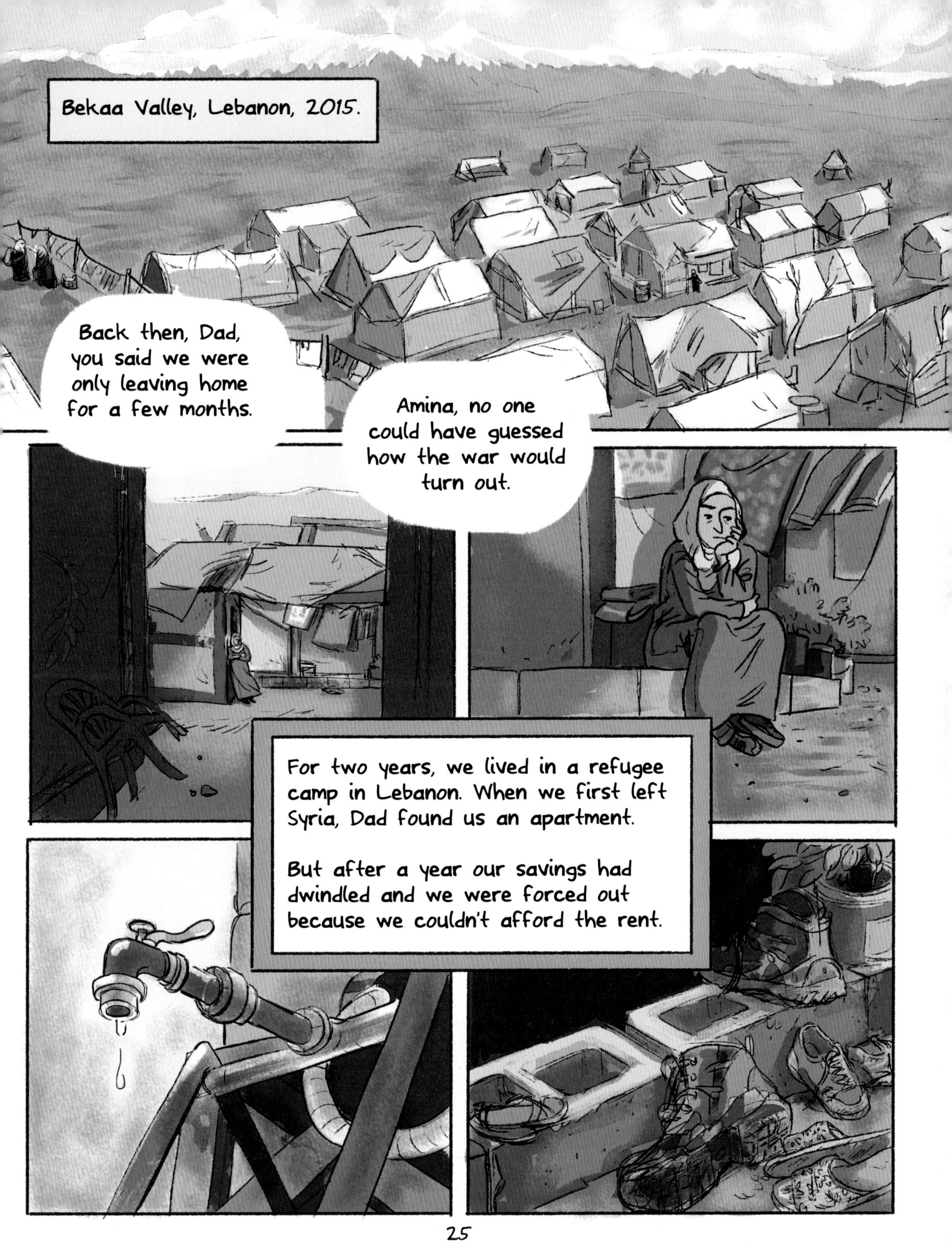
Bekaa Valley, Lebanon, 2015.
Back then, Dad, you said we were only leaving home for a few months.
Amina, no one could have guessed how the war would turn out.
For two years, we lived in a refugee camp in Lebanon. When we first left Syria, Dad found us an apartment.
But after a year our savings had dwindled and we were forced out because we couldn't afford the rent.

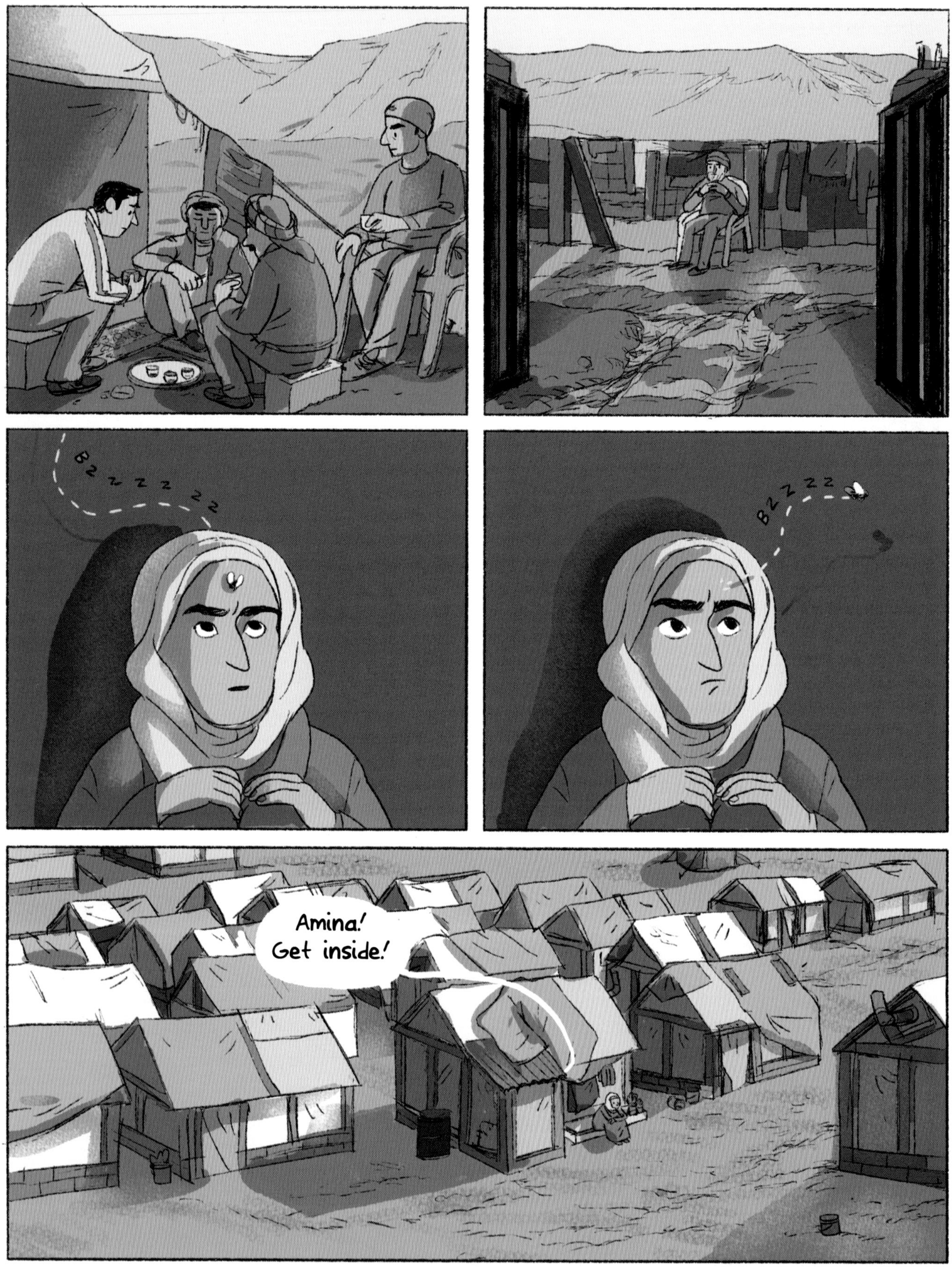
BZZZZZZ
BZZZZ
Amina! Get inside!

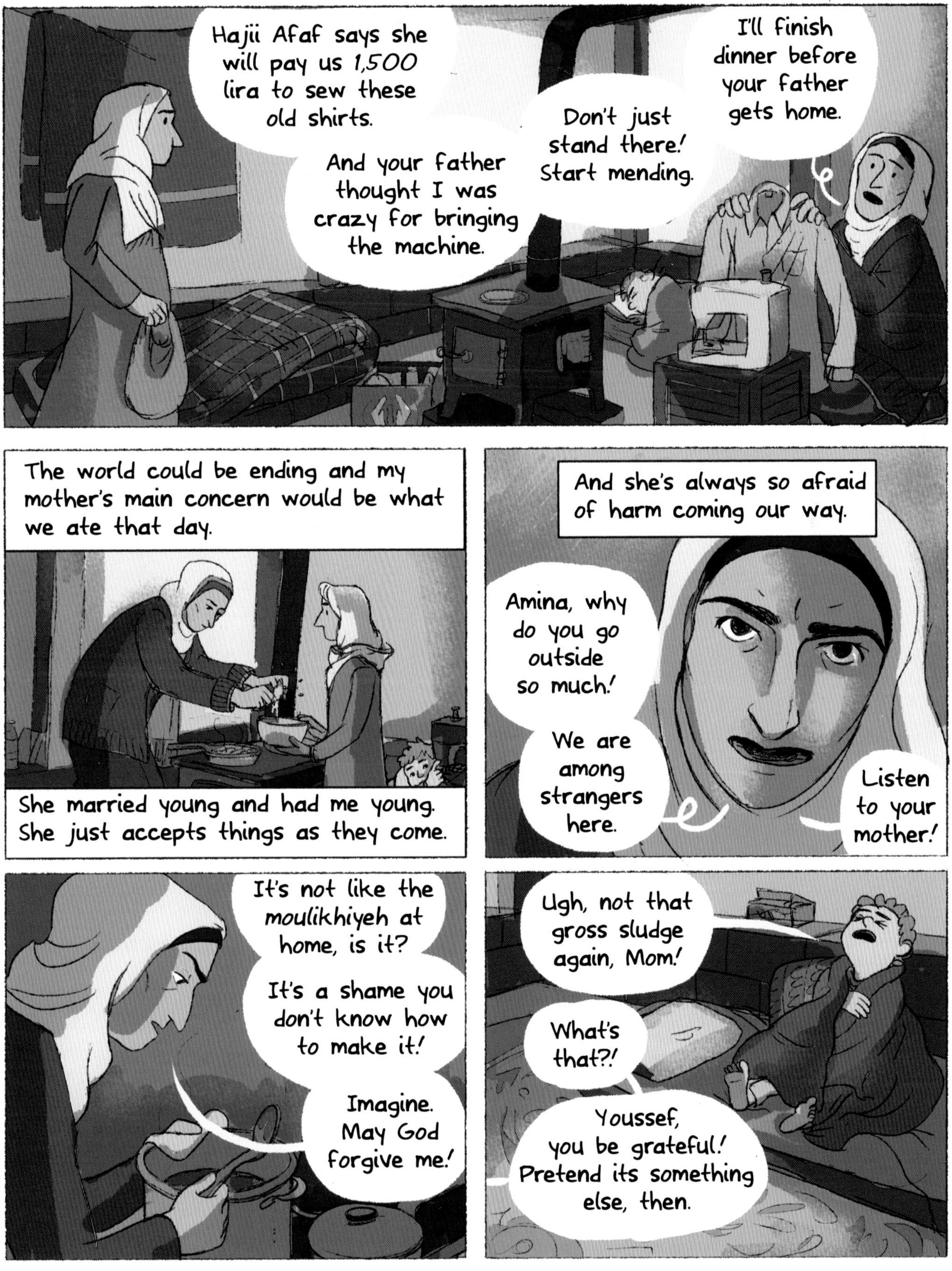
Hajii Afaf says she will pay us 1,500 lira to sew these old shirts.
And your father thought I was crazy for bringing the machine.
Don't just stand there! Start mending.
I'll finish dinner before your father gets home.
The world could be ending and my mother's main concern would be what we ate that day.
She married young and had me young. She just accepts things as they come.
And she's always so afraid of harm coming our way.
Amina, why do you go outside so much!
We are among strangers here.
Listen to your mother!
It's not like the moulikhiyeh at home, is it?
It's a shame you don't know how to make it!
Imagine. May God forgive me!
Ugh, not that gross sludge again, Mom!
What's that?!
Youssef, you be grateful! Pretend its something else, then.

Aleppo City, Syria, 2011.

My mother would work all day, carving eggplants and zucchini — chopping and peeling.

All for the guests.

Dalia, you've outdone yourself!

Before the war, Dad had a big shoemaking business.

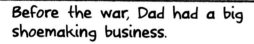

He was always traveling — to China, to Russia, even to Europe.

Dalia, the tea?

Right here, husband.

Don't get the floor muddy!

Bekaa Valley, Lebanon, 2015.

What difference does it make, wife?

28

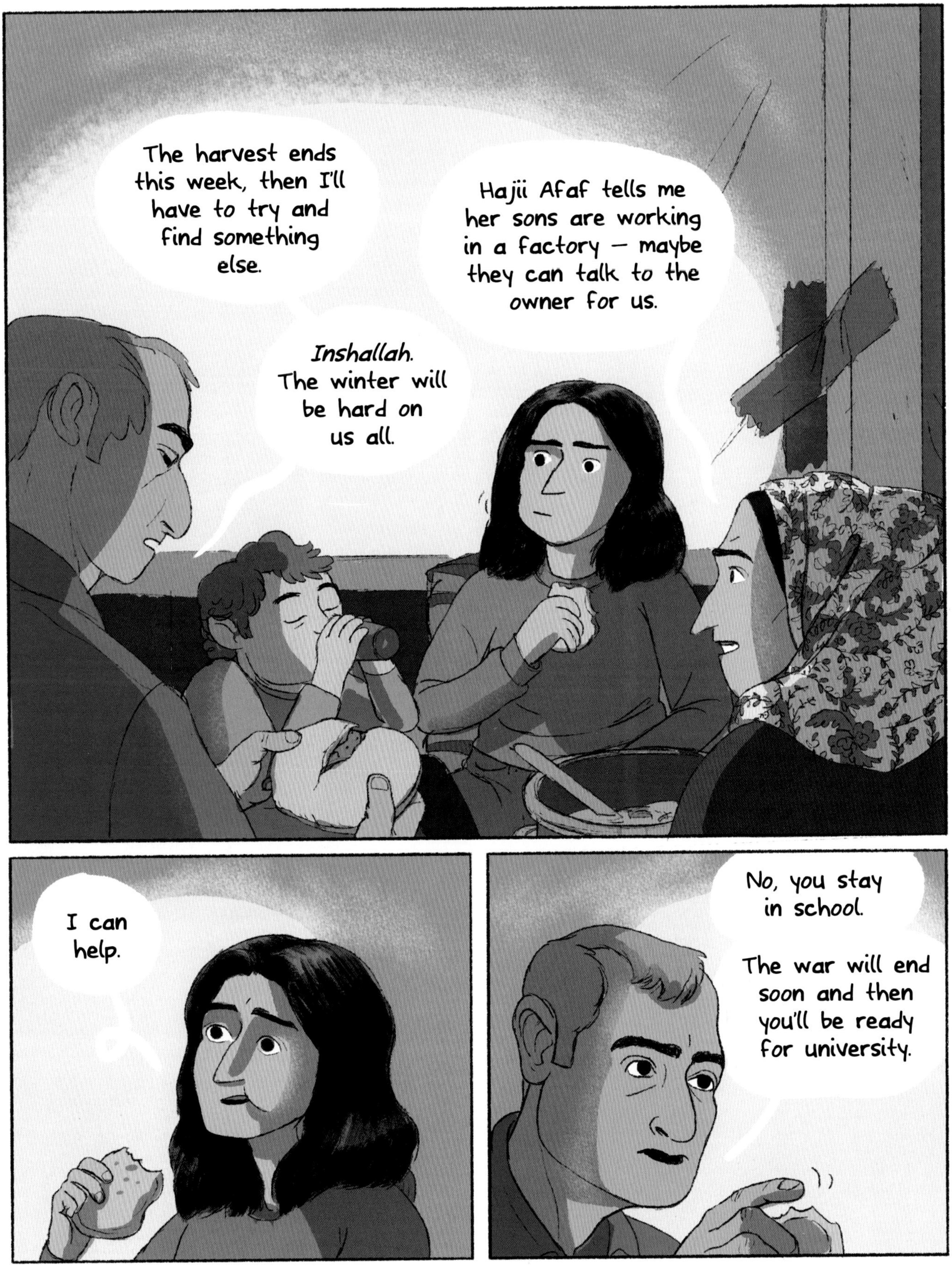
The harvest ends this week, then I'll have to try and find something else.
Hajii Afaf tells me her sons are working in a factory — maybe they can talk to the owner for us.
Inshallah. The winter will be hard on us all.
I can help.
No, you stay in school.
The war will end soon and then you'll be ready for university.

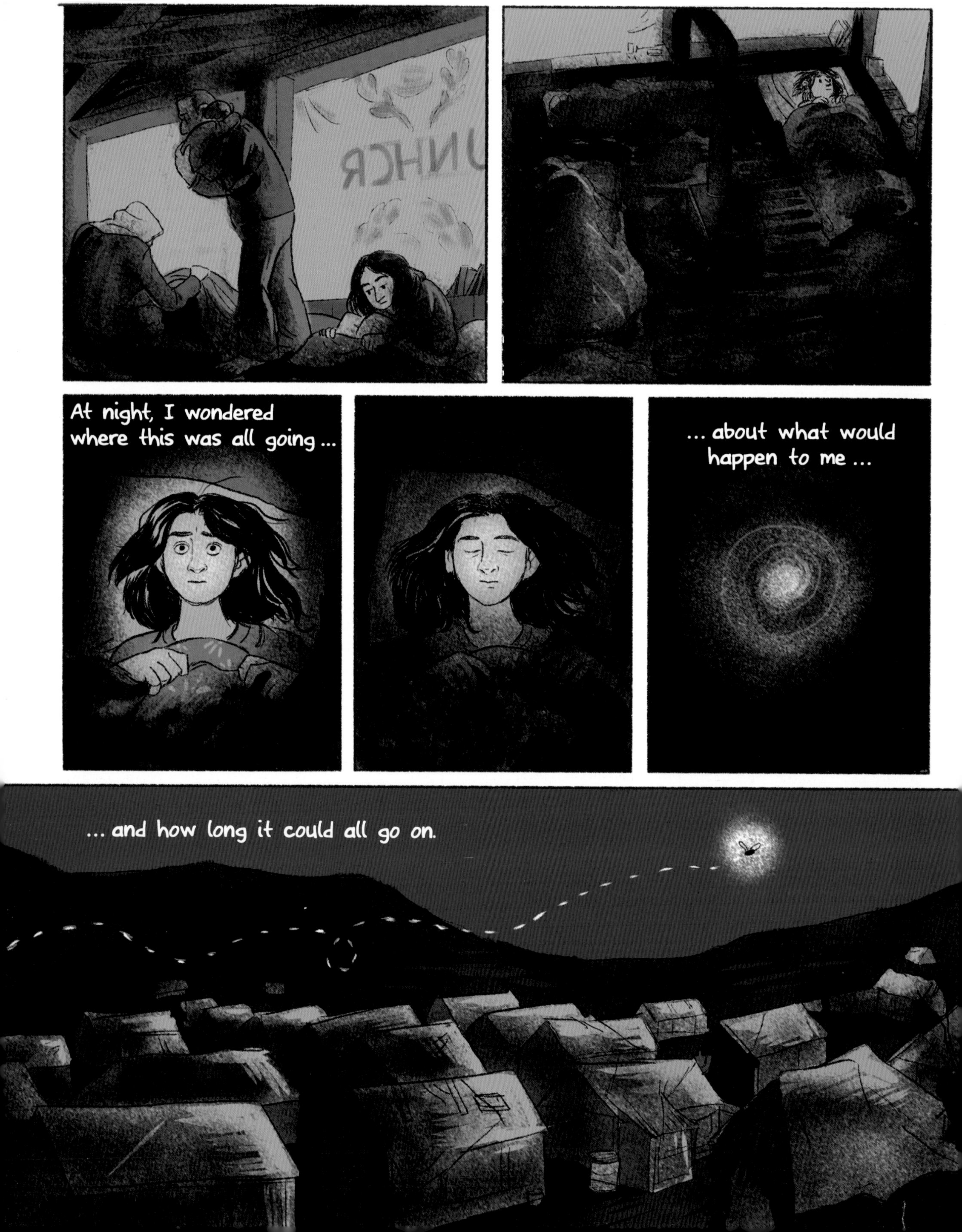
UNHCR
At night, I wondered where this was all going ...
... about what would happen to me ...
... and how long it could all go on.

More than four million Syrians fled their homes, just like we did.

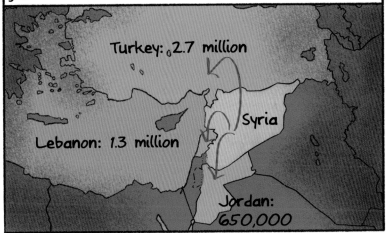

Turkey: 2.7 million

Lebanon: 1.3 million

Syria

Jordan: 650,000

The host countries struggled to manage the crush of refugees and the UNHCR was billions of dollars short in humanitarian assistance.

Dad couldn't find steady work, so we had to cut costs where we could. We stopped buying meat.

The Lebanese government was weak and divided. They couldn't come to an agreement about what to do.

See, a few decades ago Lebanon had suffered a 15-year civil war after Palestinians fled there from Israel.

The Syrians now crowding into Lebanon ignited fears of a new war.

So instead of allowing Syrians to integrate into Lebanese society, they were kept separate.

Syrians can't build homes.

Syrians can't work legally.

Syrians must renew their residency every year.

TIOR

LABOR

DEFE

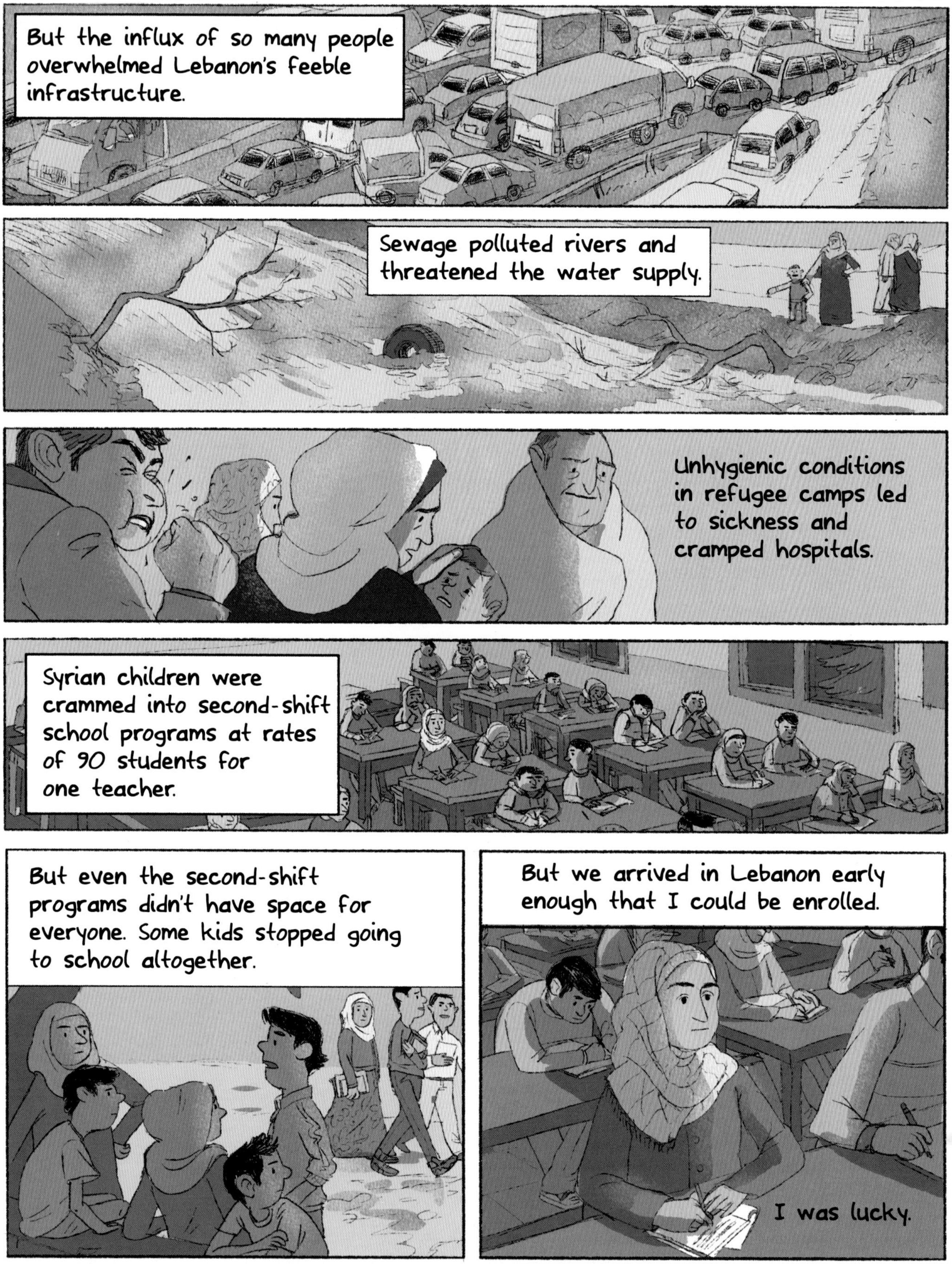
But the influx of so many people overwhelmed Lebanon's feeble infrastructure.
Sewage polluted rivers and threatened the water supply.
Unhygienic conditions in refugee camps led to sickness and cramped hospitals.
Syrian children were crammed into second-shift school programs at rates of 90 students for one teacher.
But even the second-shift programs didn't have space for everyone. Some kids stopped going to school altogether.
But we arrived in Lebanon early enough that I could be enrolled.
I was lucky.

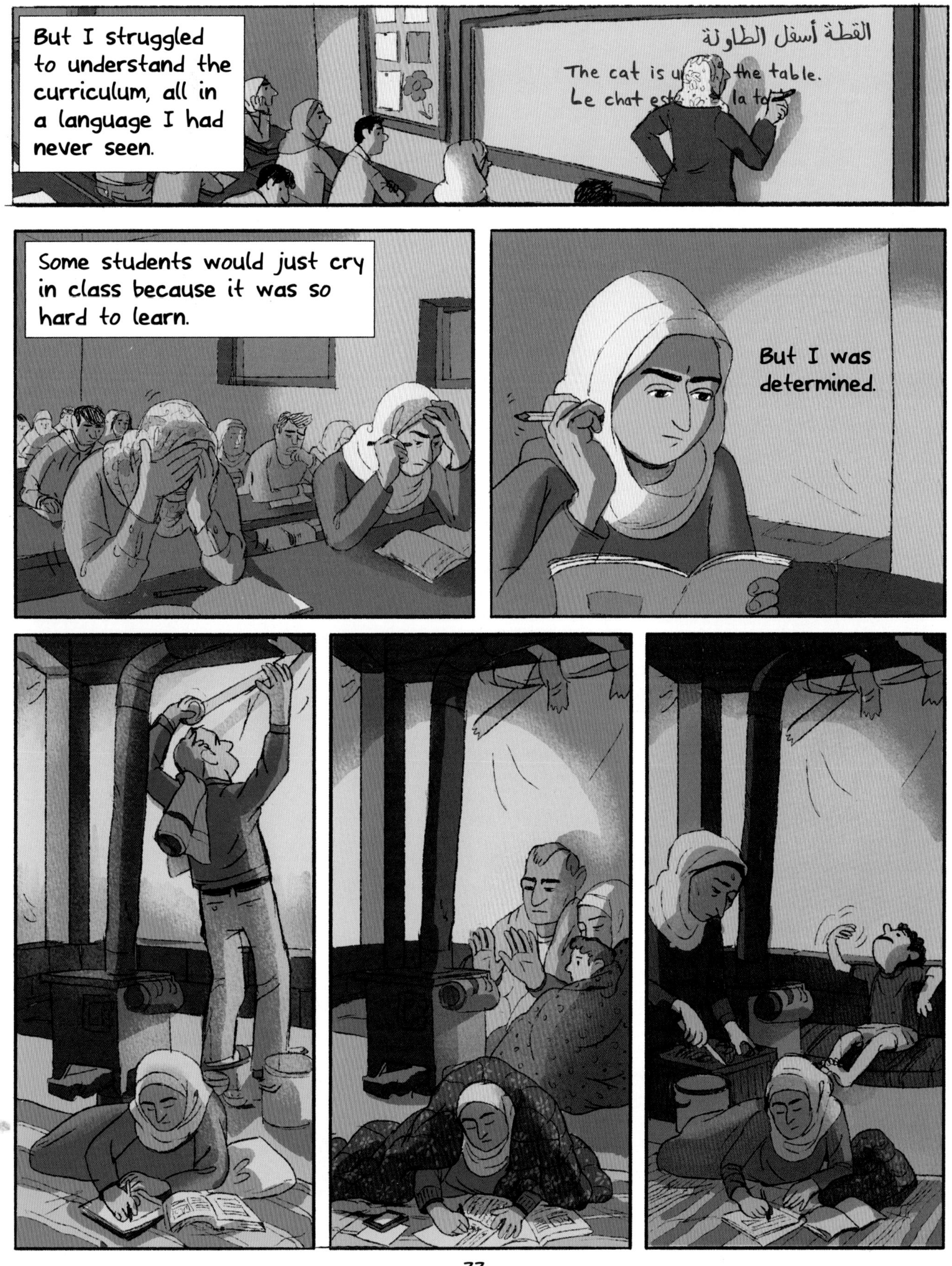
But I struggled to understand the curriculum, all in a language I had never seen.
القطة أسفل الطاولة
The cat is u the table.
Le chat est la ta
Some students would just cry in class because it was so hard to learn.
But I was determined.

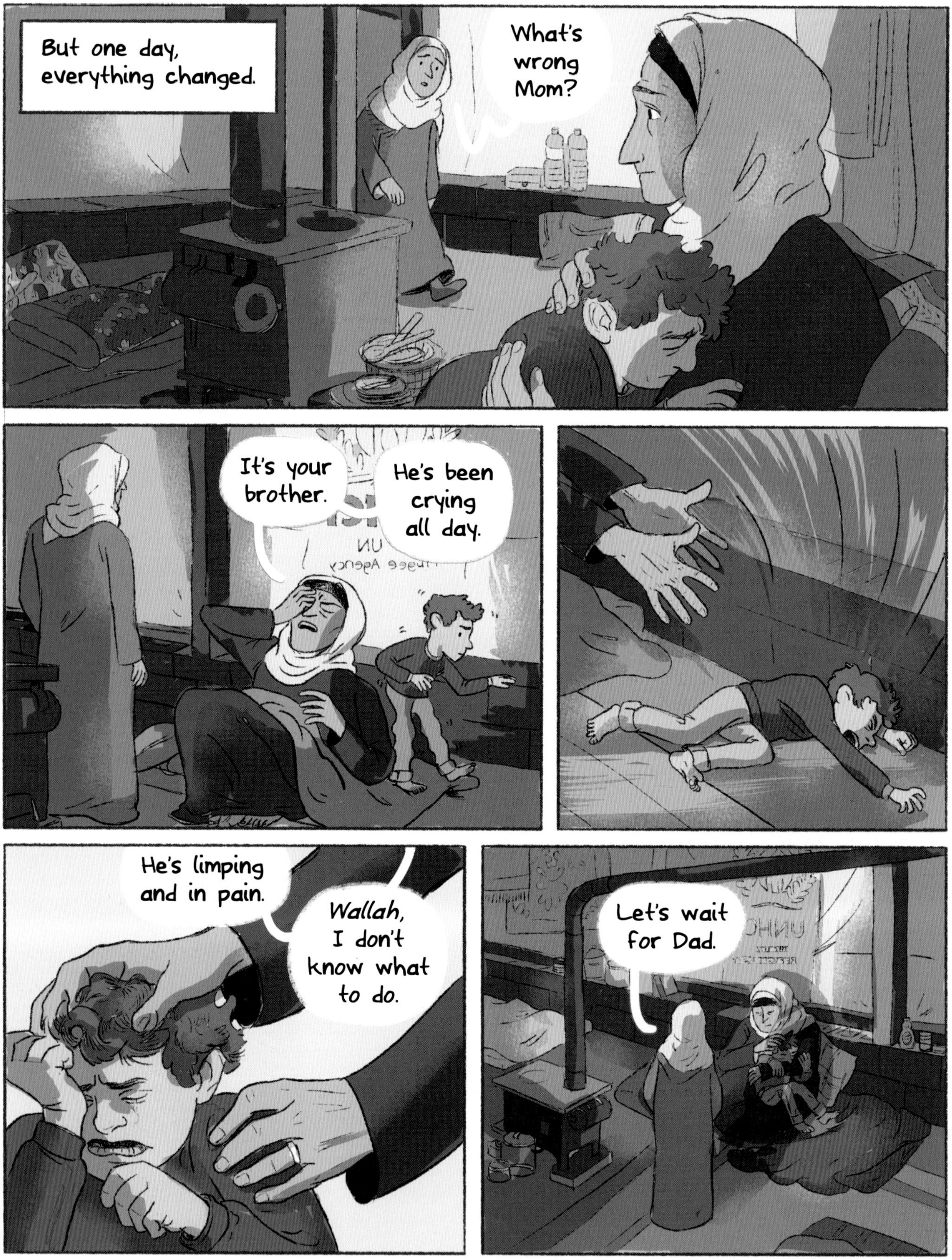
But one day, everything changed.
What's wrong Mom?
It's your brother.
He's been crying all day.
He's limping and in pain.
Wallah, I don't know what to do.
Let's wait for Dad.

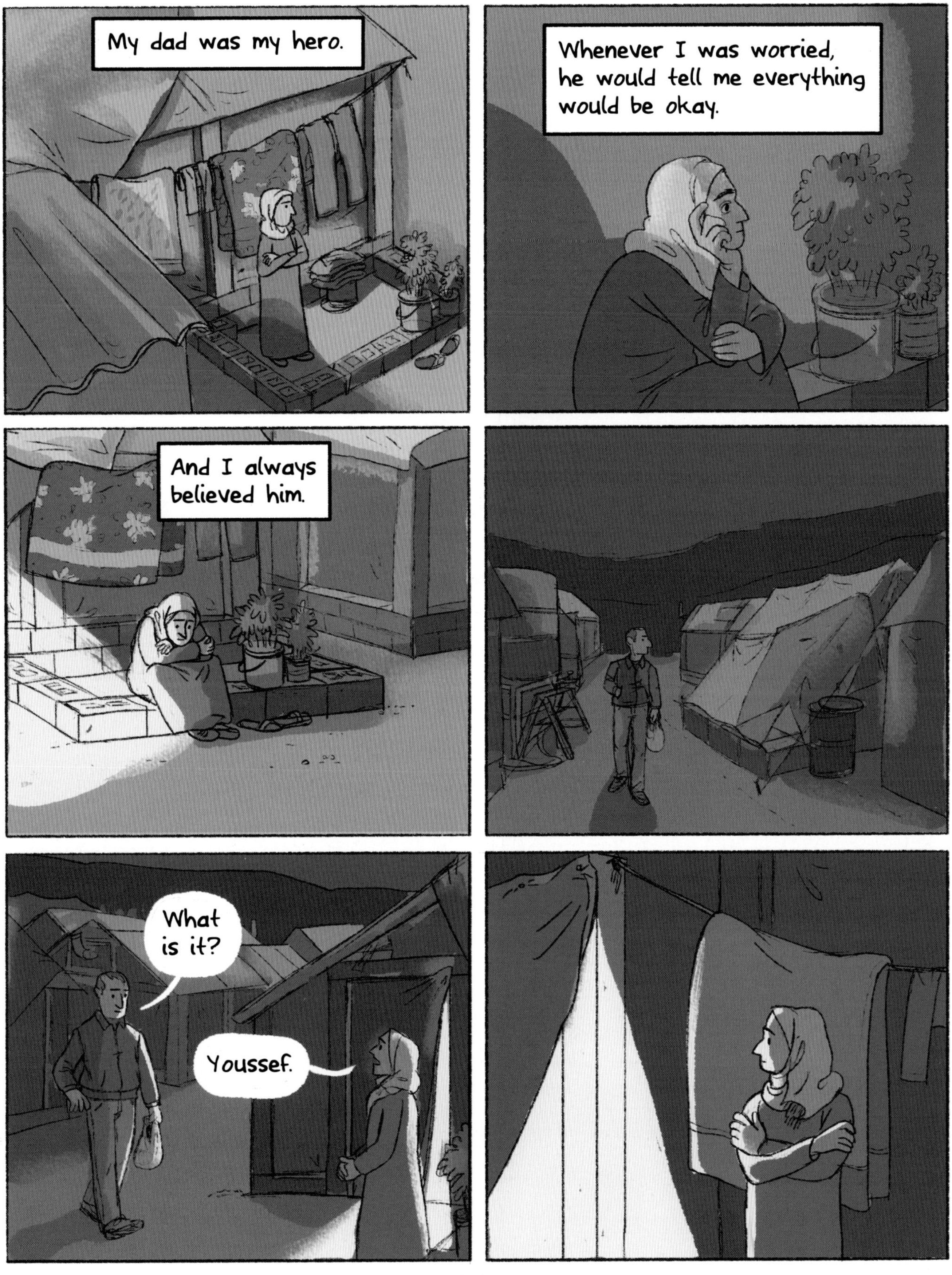
My dad was my hero.
Whenever I was worried, he would tell me everything would be okay.
And I always believed him.
What is it?
Youssef.

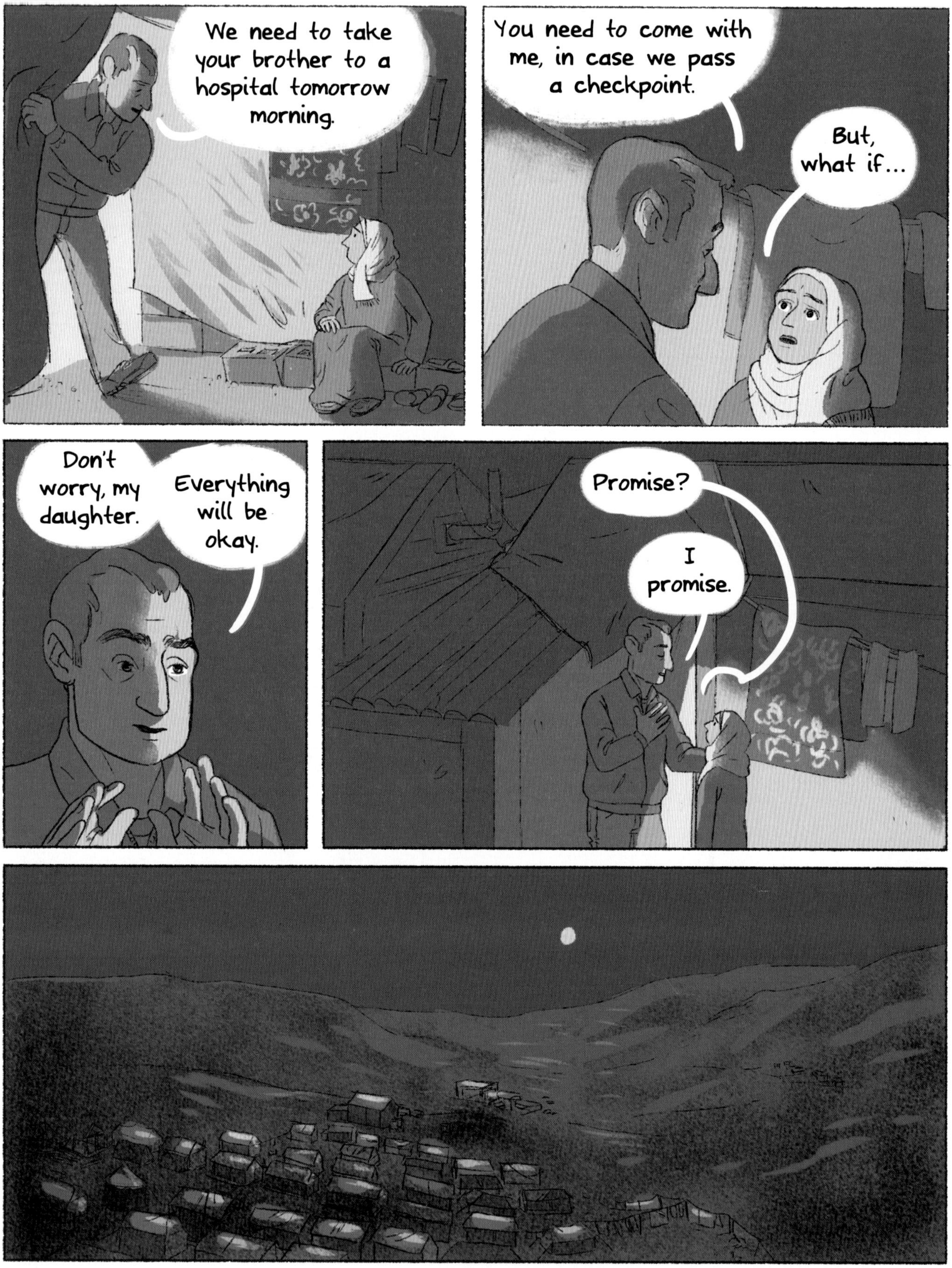
We need to take your brother to a hospital tomorrow morning.
You need to come with me, in case we pass a checkpoint.
But, what if...
Don't worry, my daughter.
Everything will be okay.
Promise?
I promise.

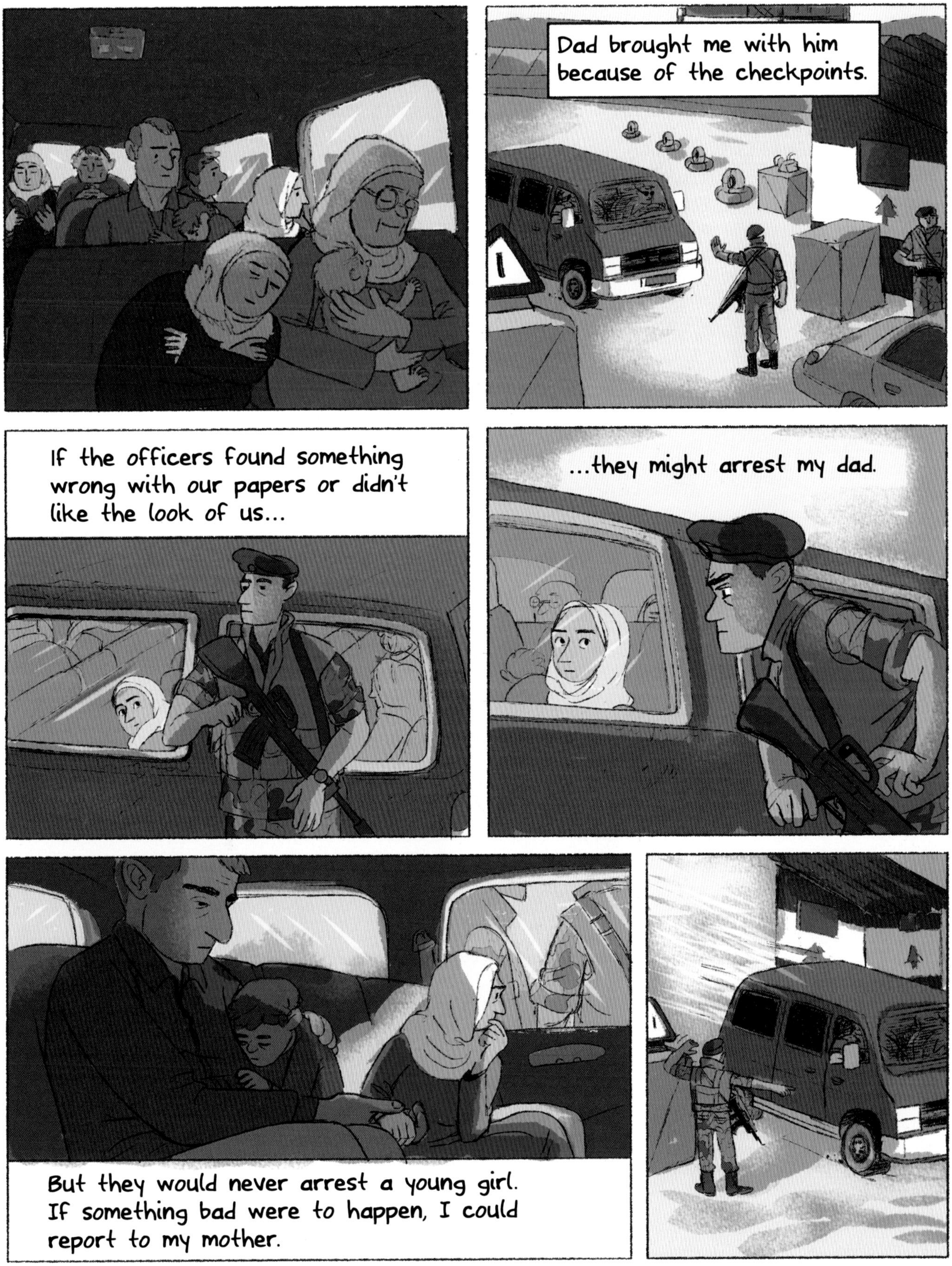

Dad brought me with him because of the checkpoints.
If the officers found something wrong with our papers or didn't like the look of us...
...they might arrest my dad.
But they would never arrest a young girl. If something bad were to happen, I could report to my mother.

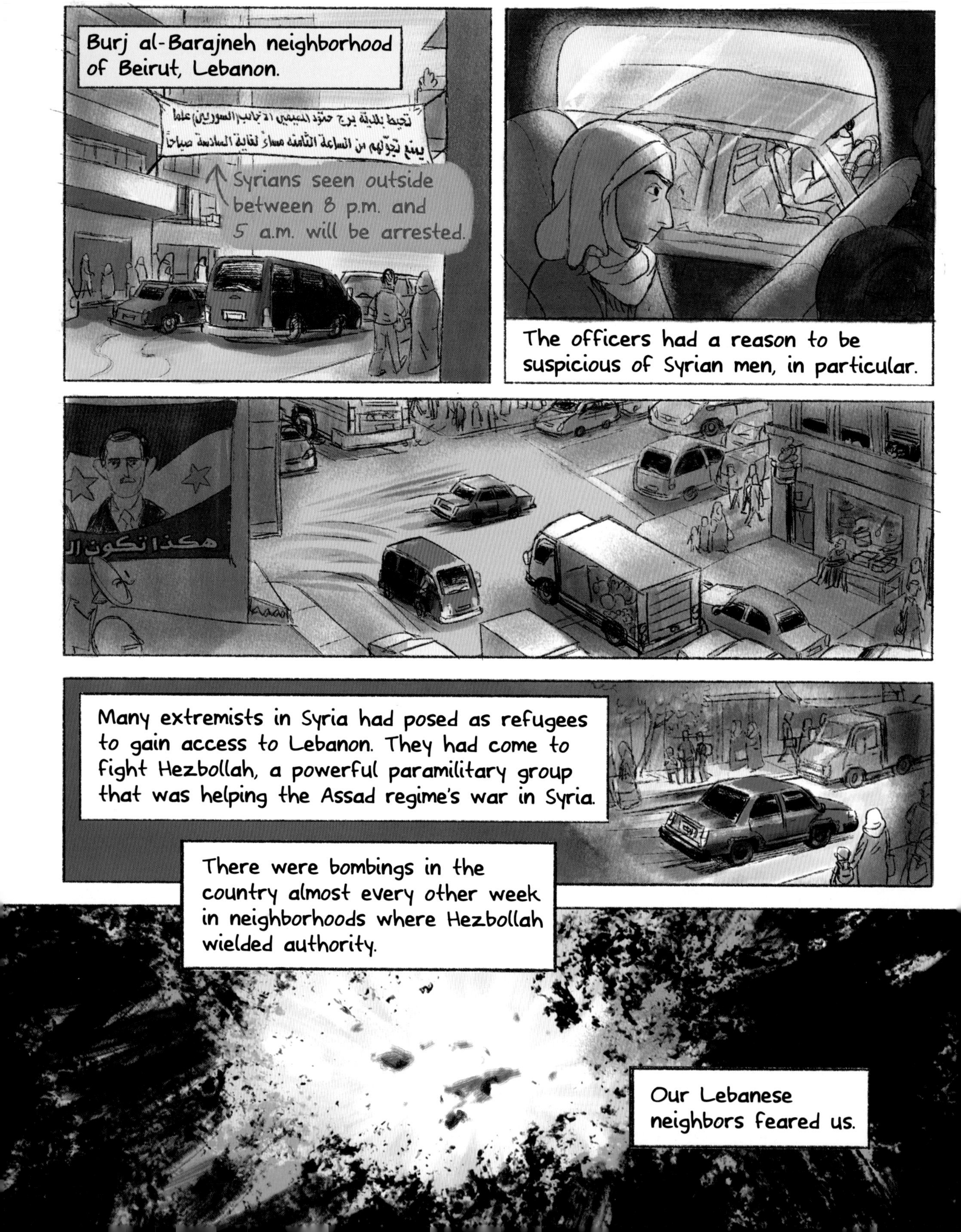

Burj al-Barajneh neighborhood of Beirut, Lebanon.
تحيط بلدية برج حمود المقيمين الاجانب (السوريين) علما
يمنع تجولهم من الساعة الثامنة مساءً لغاية السادسة صباحاً
Syrians seen outside between 8 p.m. and 5 a.m. will be arrested.
The officers had a reason to be suspicious of Syrian men, in particular.
هكذا تكون ال
Many extremists in Syria had posed as refugees to gain access to Lebanon. They had come to fight Hezbollah, a powerful paramilitary group that was helping the Assad regime's war in Syria.
There were bombings in the country almost every other week in neighborhoods where Hezbollah wielded authority.
Our Lebanese neighbors feared us.

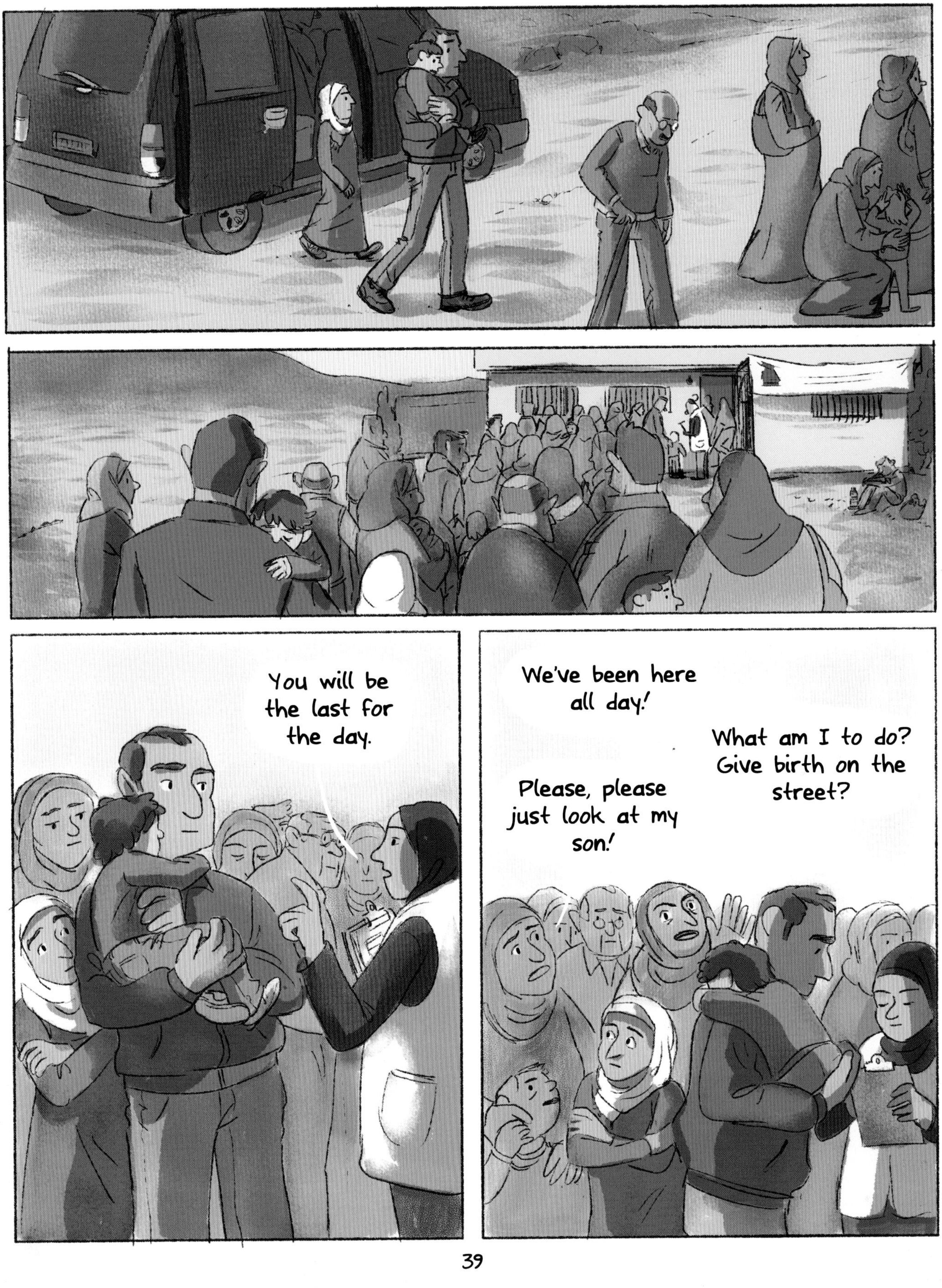
You will be the last for the day.
We've been here all day!
Please, please just look at my son!
What am I to do? Give birth on the street?

Your child has bacterial meningitis.

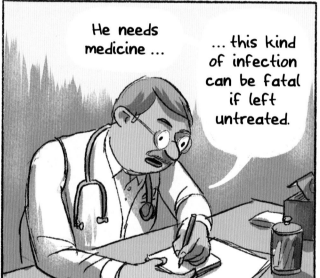
He needs medicine ...

... this kind of infection can be fatal if left untreated.

Fatal?

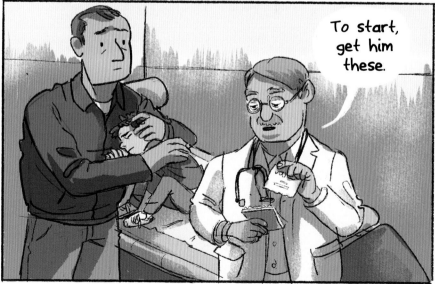
To start, get him these.

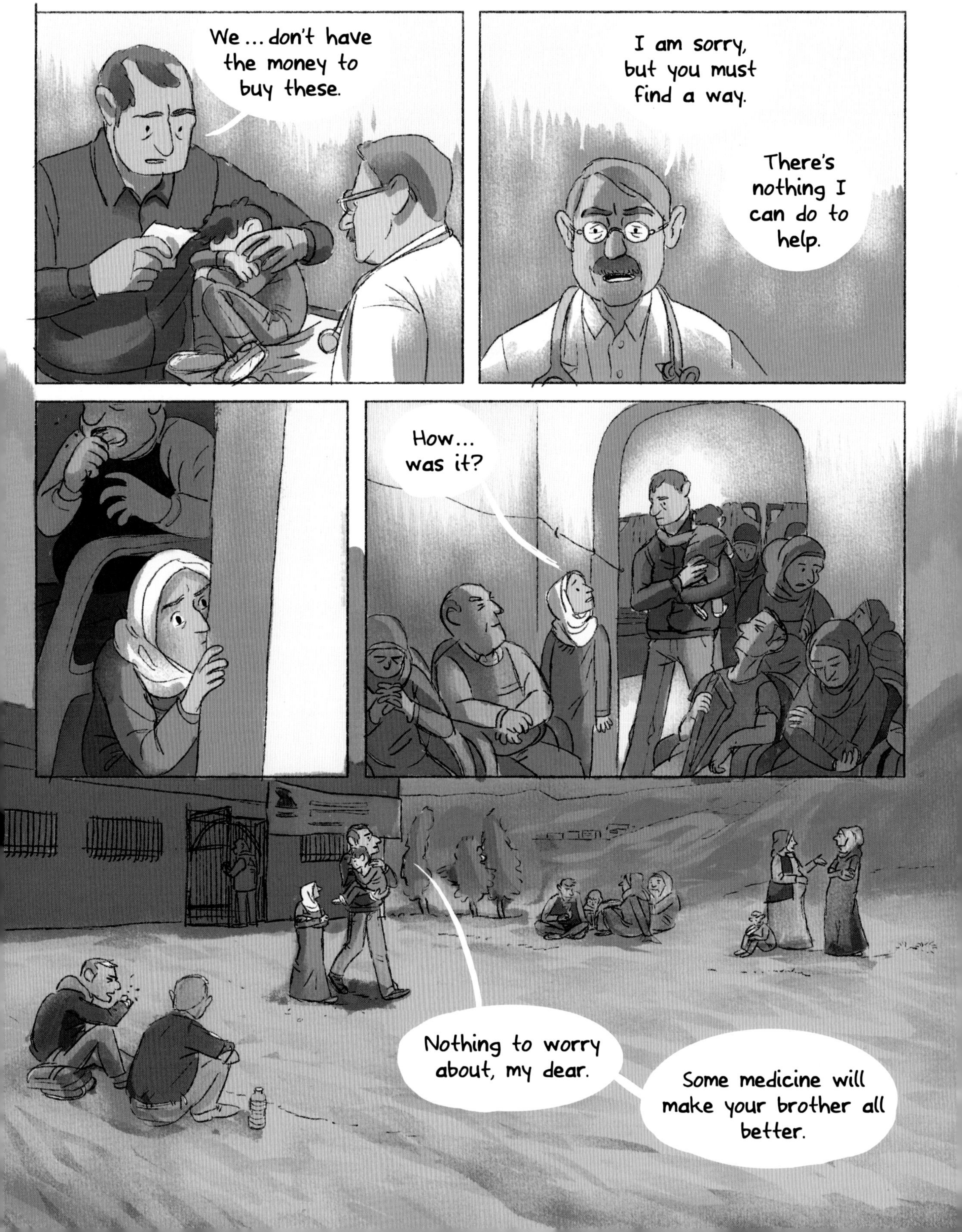
We ... don't have the money to buy these.
I am sorry, but you must find a way.
There's nothing I can do to help.
How... was it?
Nothing to worry about, my dear.
Some medicine will make your brother all better.

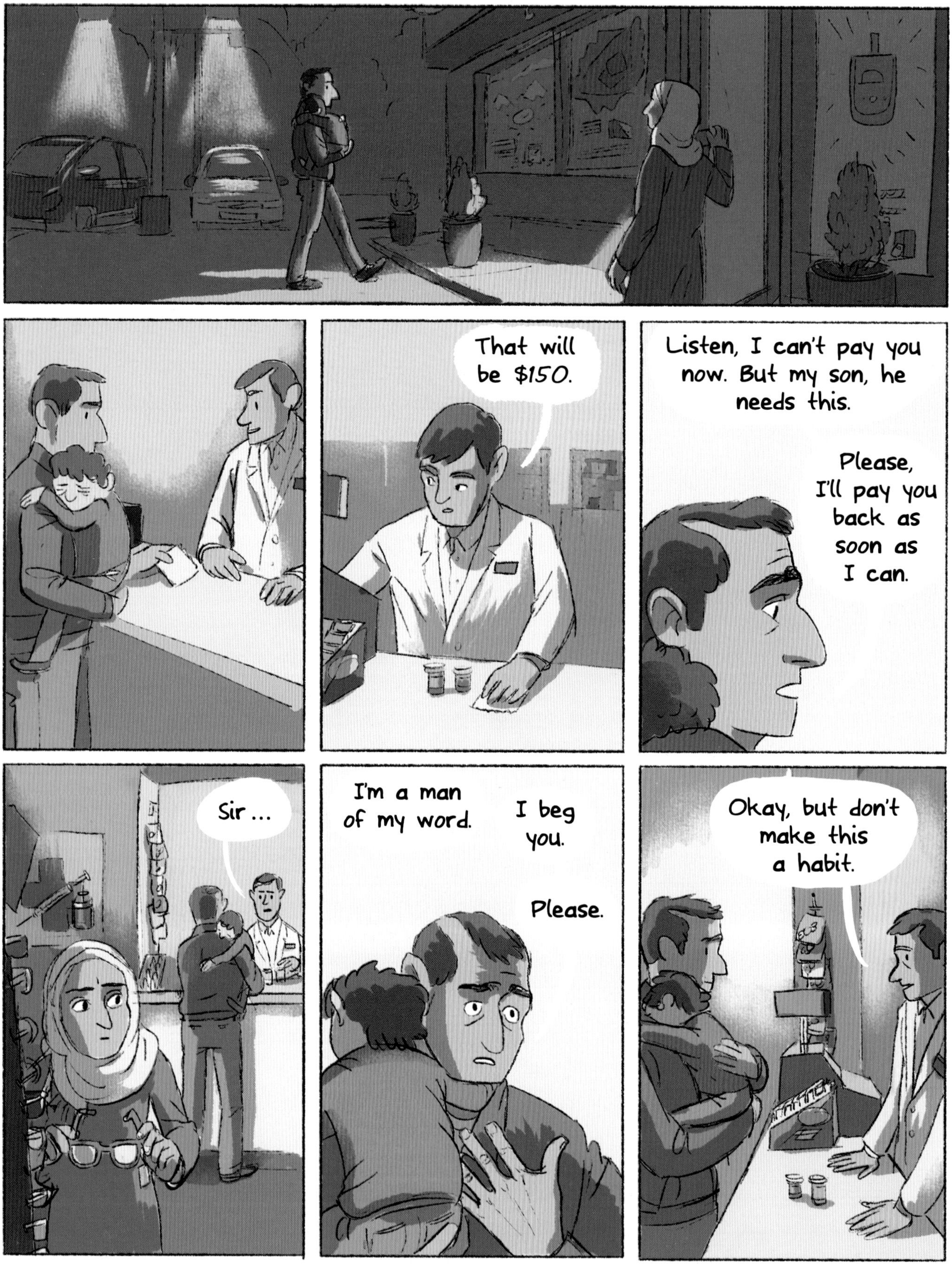
That will be $150.
Listen, I can't pay you now. But my son, he needs this.
Please, I'll pay you back as soon as I can.
Sir ...
I'm a man of my word.
I beg you.
Please.
Okay, but don't make this a habit.

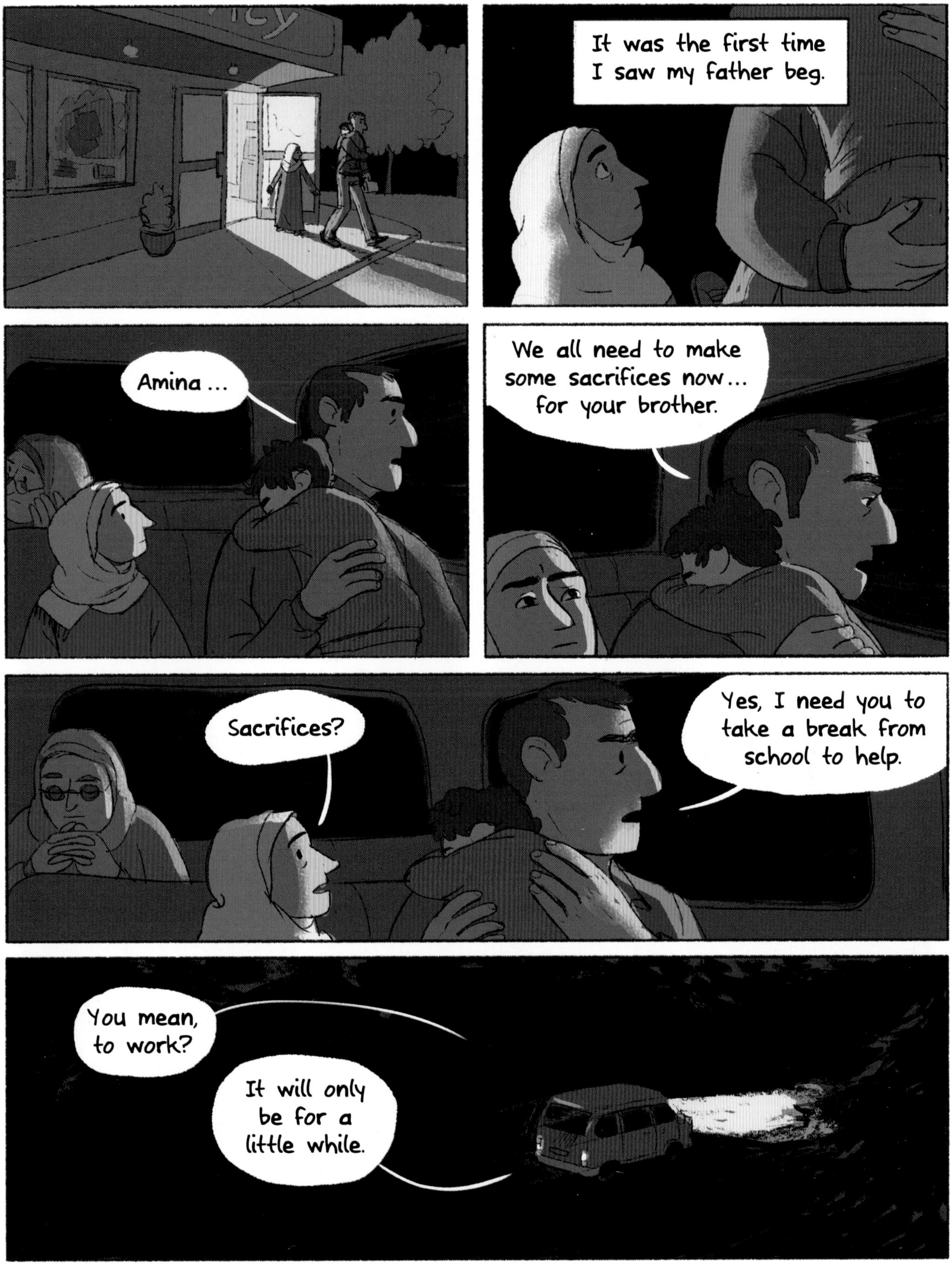
It was the first time I saw my father beg.
Amina ...
We all need to make some sacrifices now... for your brother.
Sacrifices?
Yes, I need you to take a break from school to help.
You mean, to work?
It will only be for a little while.

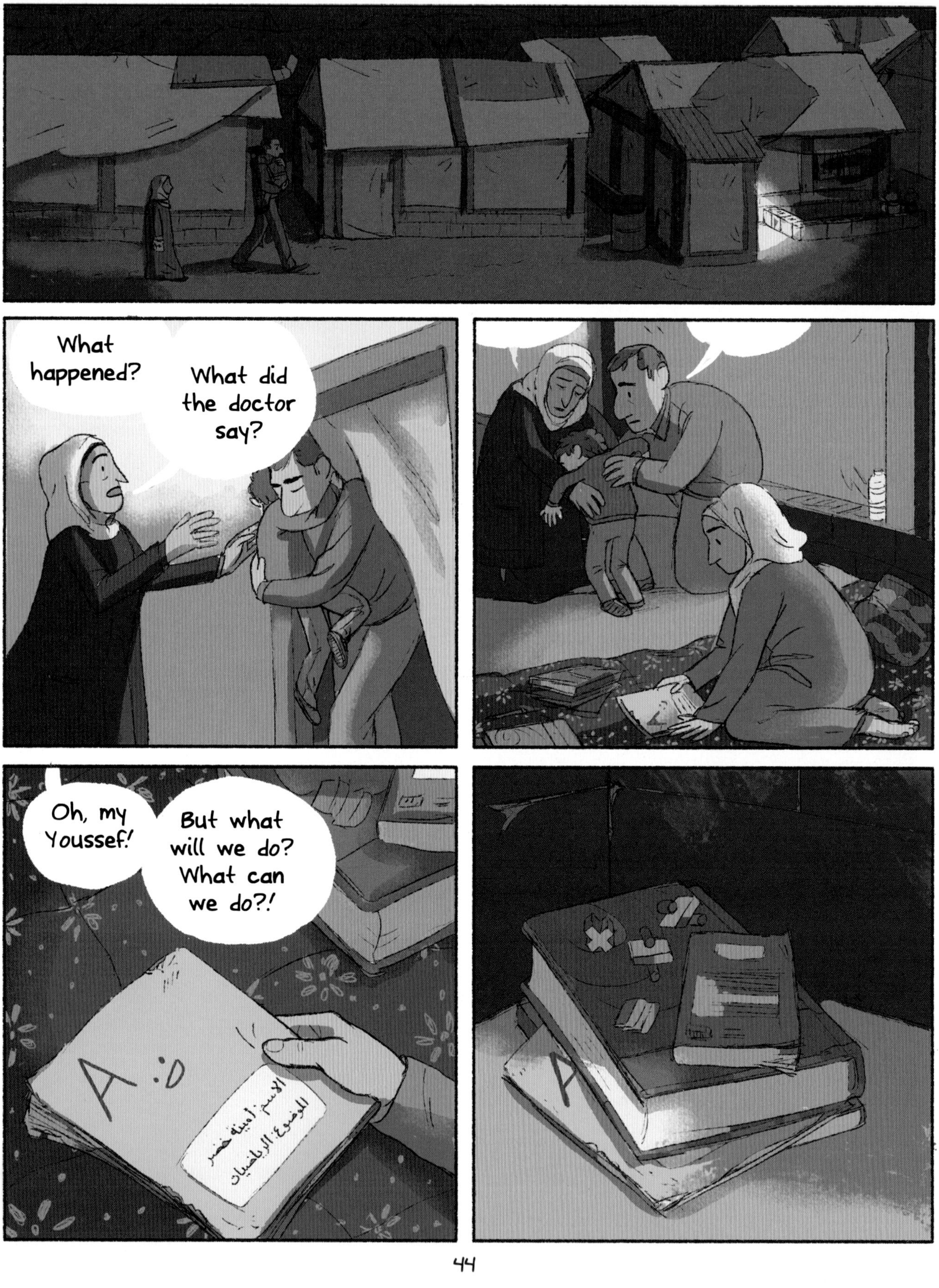
What happened?
What did the doctor say?
Oh, my Youssef!
But what will we do? What can we do?!
A :D
الاسم: أمينة خضر
الموضوع: الرياضيات

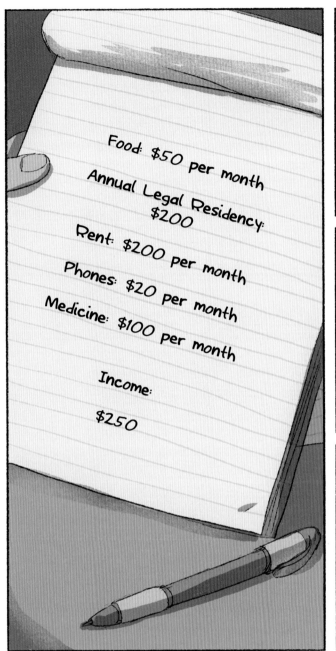

Food: $50 per month

Annual Legal Residency: $200

Rent: $200 per month

Phones: $20 per month

Medicine: $100 per month

Income:

$250

How will we manage this?

Amina will work. That should at least cover the cost of food.

But it won't be enough.

What will happen when the pharmacist asks for what we owe?

What will we do then?

I will stop renewing my Lebanese residency papers. That will save us $200 a year.

What are you saying? Don't you know what that means?!

It meant that Dad became an illegal resident of Lebanon.

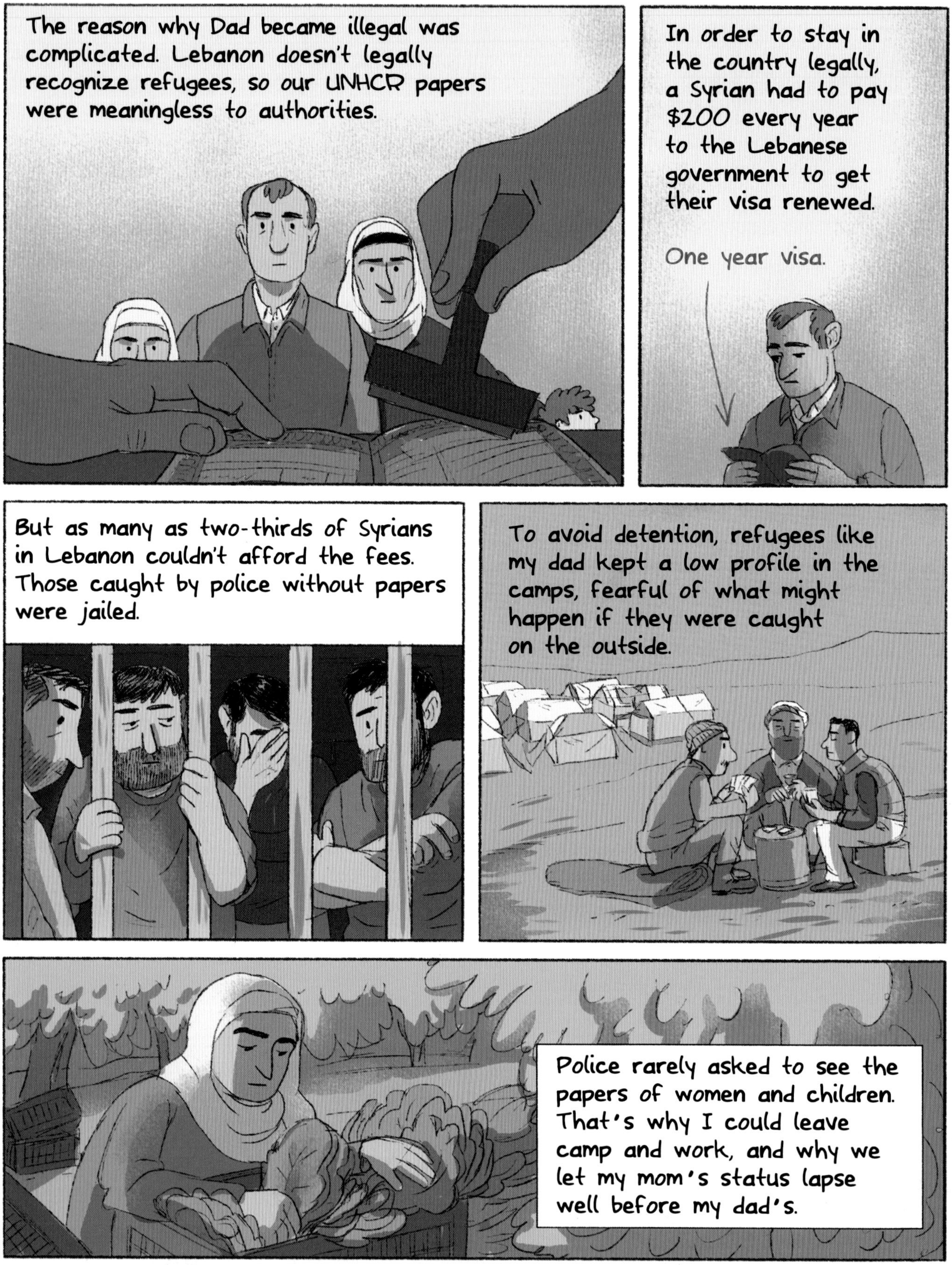
The reason why Dad became illegal was complicated. Lebanon doesn't legally recognize refugees, so our UNHCR papers were meaningless to authorities.
In order to stay in the country legally, a Syrian had to pay $200 every year to the Lebanese government to get their visa renewed.
One year visa.
But as many as two-thirds of Syrians in Lebanon couldn't afford the fees. Those caught by police without papers were jailed.
To avoid detention, refugees like my dad kept a low profile in the camps, fearful of what might happen if they were caught on the outside.
Police rarely asked to see the papers of women and children. That's why I could leave camp and work, and why we let my mom's status lapse well before my dad's.

Dear cousin …

Dear cousin …

The armed rebellion has grown, but the lives of true Syrian revolutionaries are in danger …

Powerful Islamist and jihadist groups have emerged. They have more money and weapons than we do.

Many of my men defected to their ranks out of fear, but few really believe in their holy war.

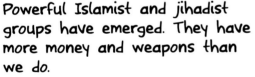

Ayn al-Arab crossing, Syria-Turkey border.

I had no choice but to flee the country. Those who've stayed are living on the edge of life, always nervous and afraid.

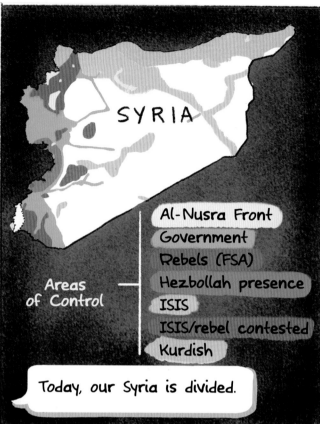

SYRIA

Areas of Control

Al-Nusra Front
Government
Rebels (FSA)
Hezbollah presence
ISIS
ISIS/rebel contested
Kurdish

Today, our Syria is divided.

Assad's sieges and starvation tactics have killed many.

My comrades across Syria are giving up on the revolution for food.

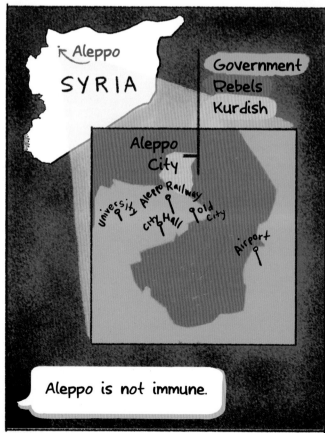

Aleppo
SYRIA

Government
Rebels
Kurdish

Aleppo City

University Aleppo Railway old city
City Hall

Airport

Aleppo is not immune.

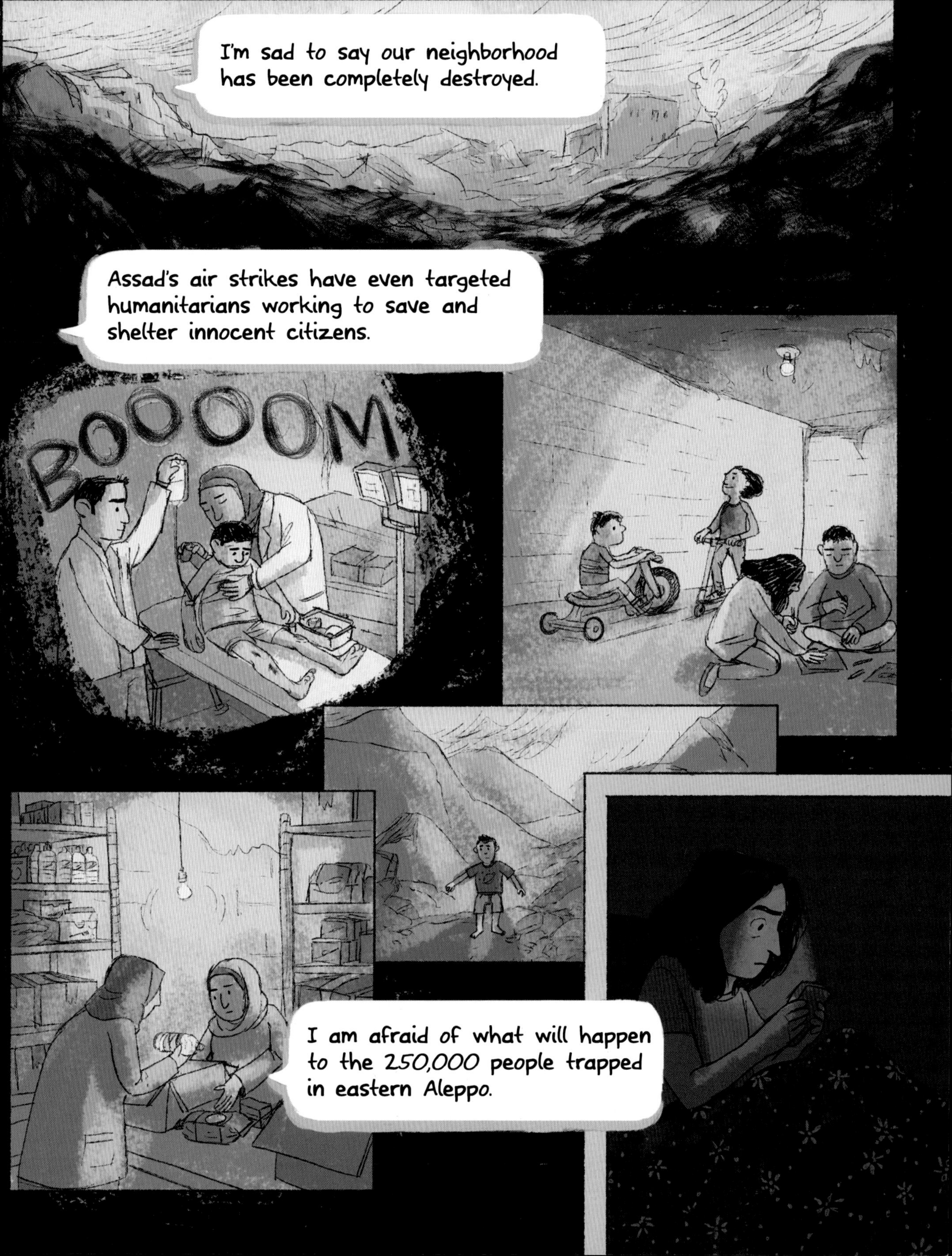
I'm sad to say our neighborhood has been completely destroyed.
Assad's air strikes have even targeted humanitarians working to save and shelter innocent citizens.
BOOOOM
I am afraid of what will happen to the 250,000 people trapped in eastern Aleppo.

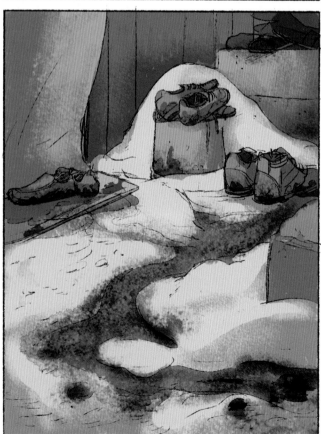

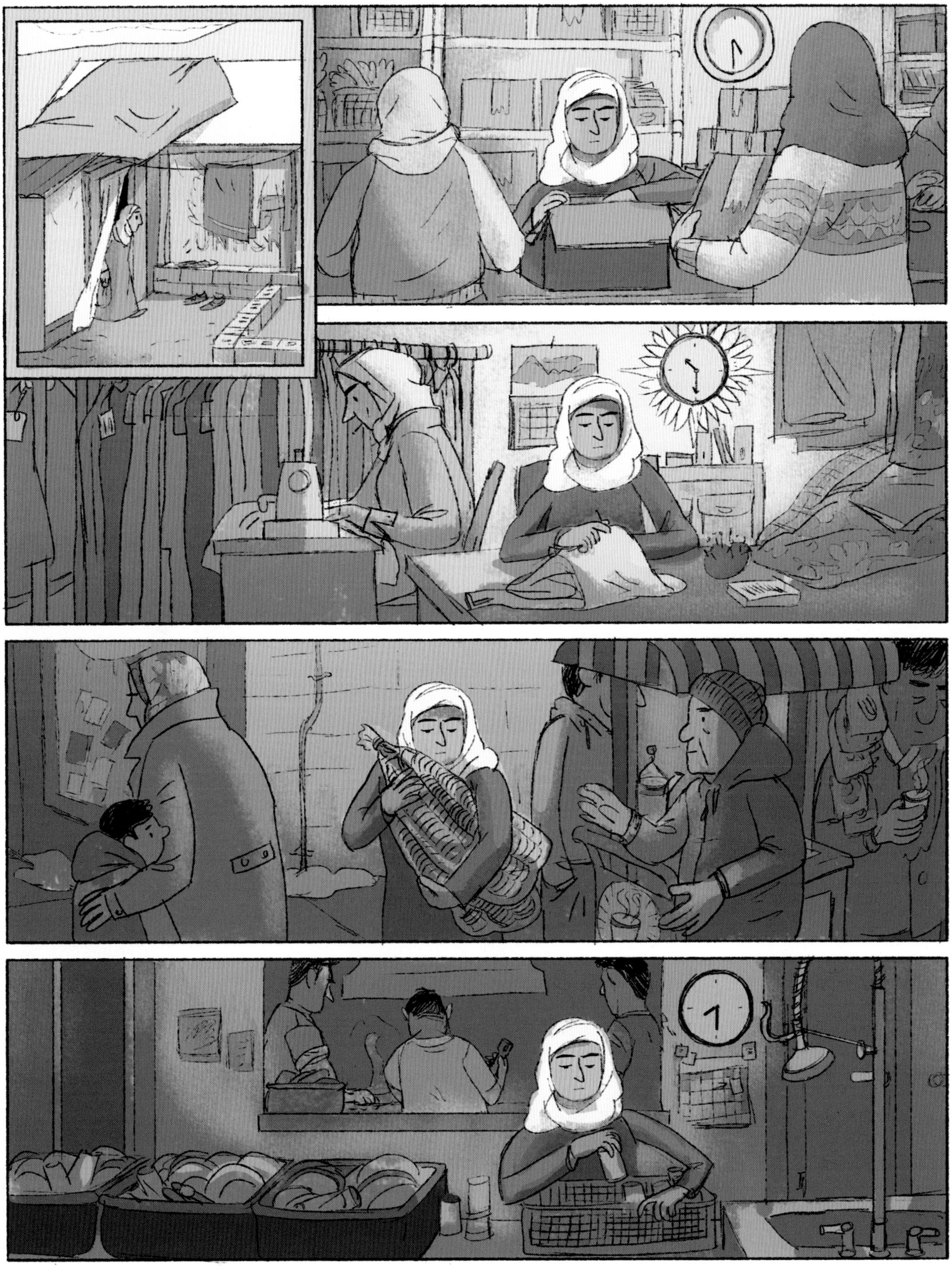

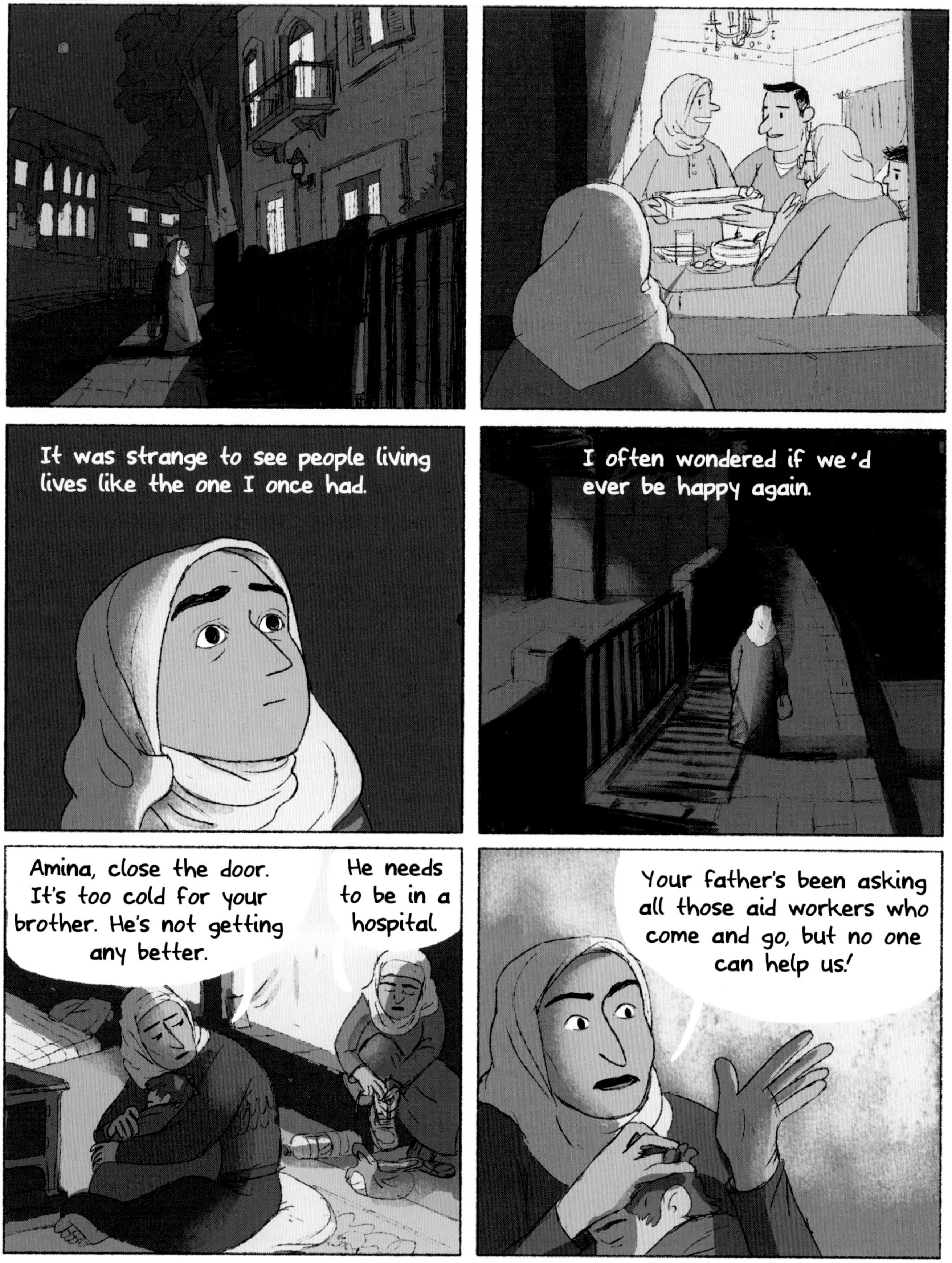
It was strange to see people living lives like the one I once had.
I often wondered if we'd ever be happy again.
Amina, close the door. It's too cold for your brother. He's not getting any better.
He needs to be in a hospital.
Your father's been asking all those aid workers who come and go, but no one can help us!

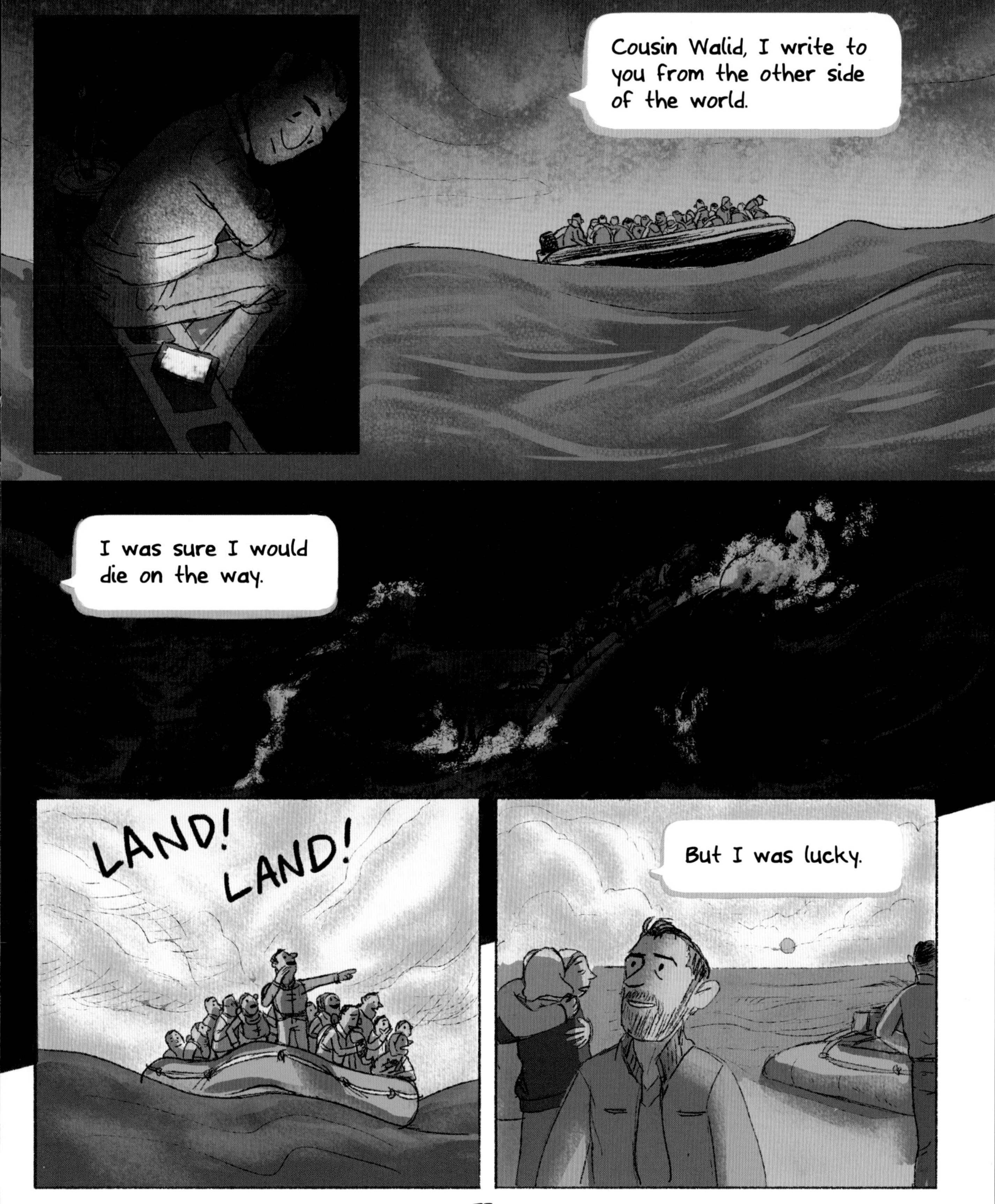
Cousin Walid, I write to you from the other side of the world.
I was sure I would die on the way.
LAND! LAND!
But I was lucky.

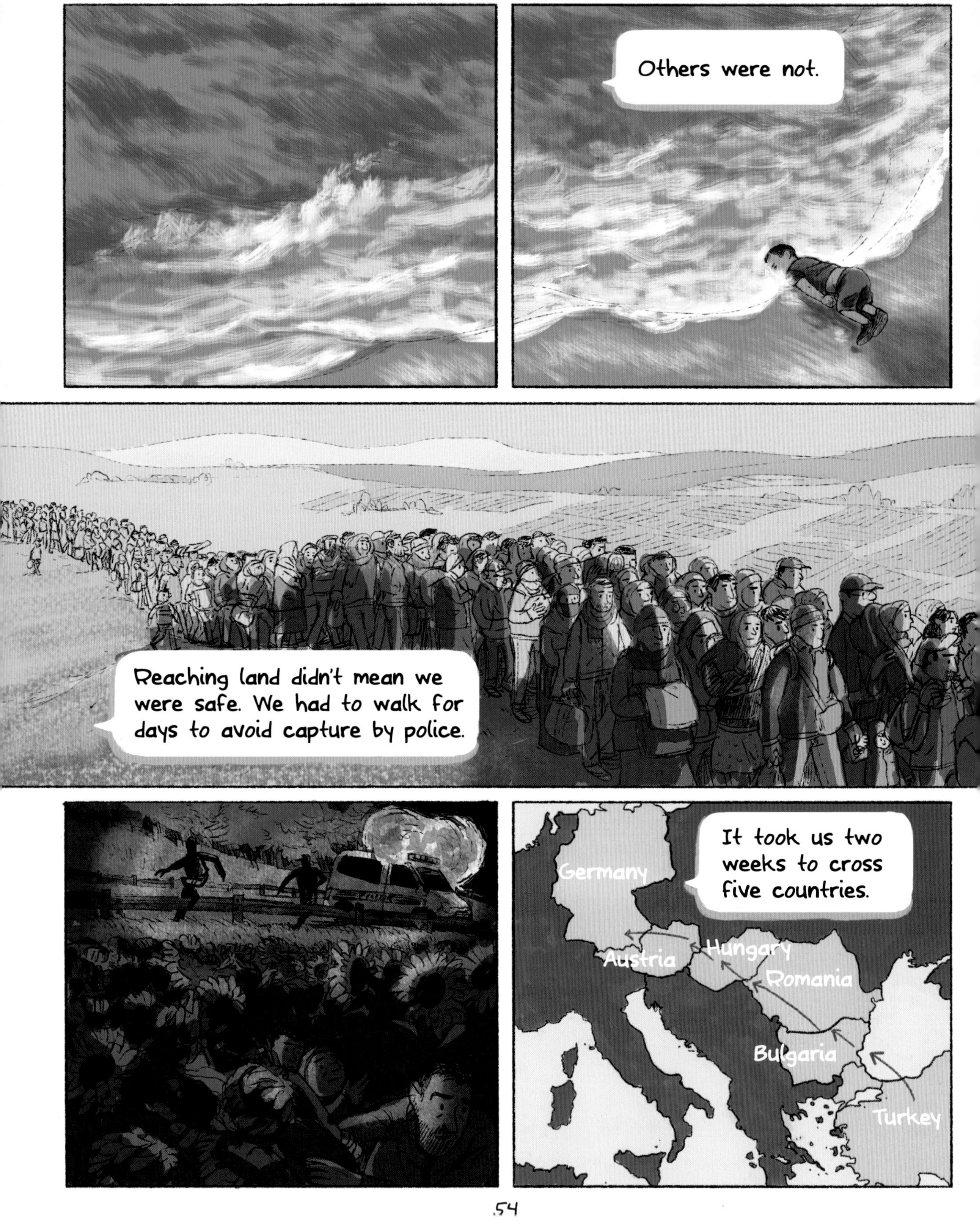
Others were not.
Reaching land didn't mean we were safe. We had to walk for days to avoid capture by police.
It took us two weeks to cross five countries.
Germany
Austria
Hungary
Romania
Bulgaria
Turkey

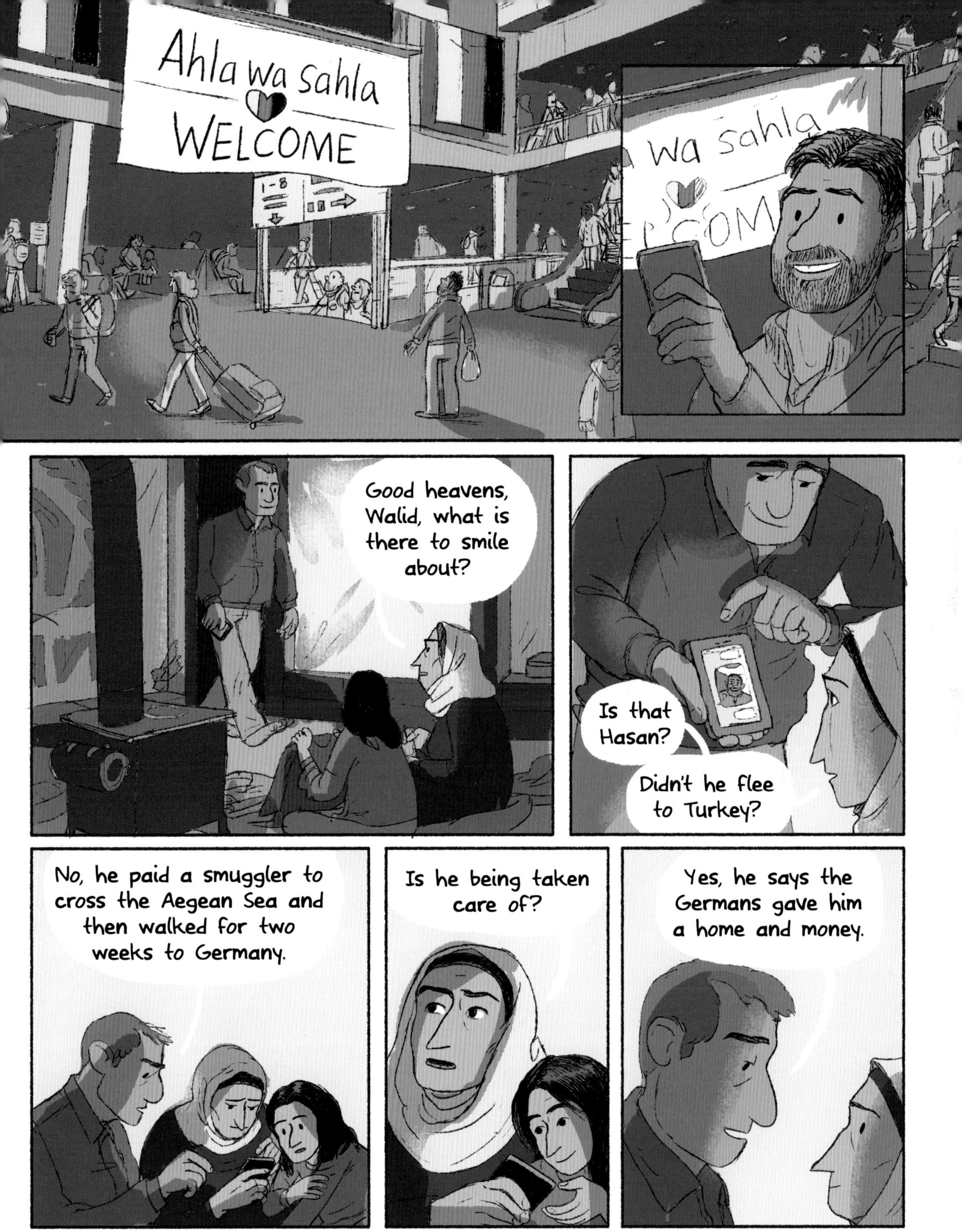
Ahla wa sahla
WELCOME
1-8
wa sahla
Good heavens, Walid, what is there to smile about?
Is that Hasan?
Didn't he flee to Turkey?
No, he paid a smuggler to cross the Aegean Sea and then walked for two weeks to Germany.
Is he being taken care of?
Yes, he says the Germans gave him a home and money.

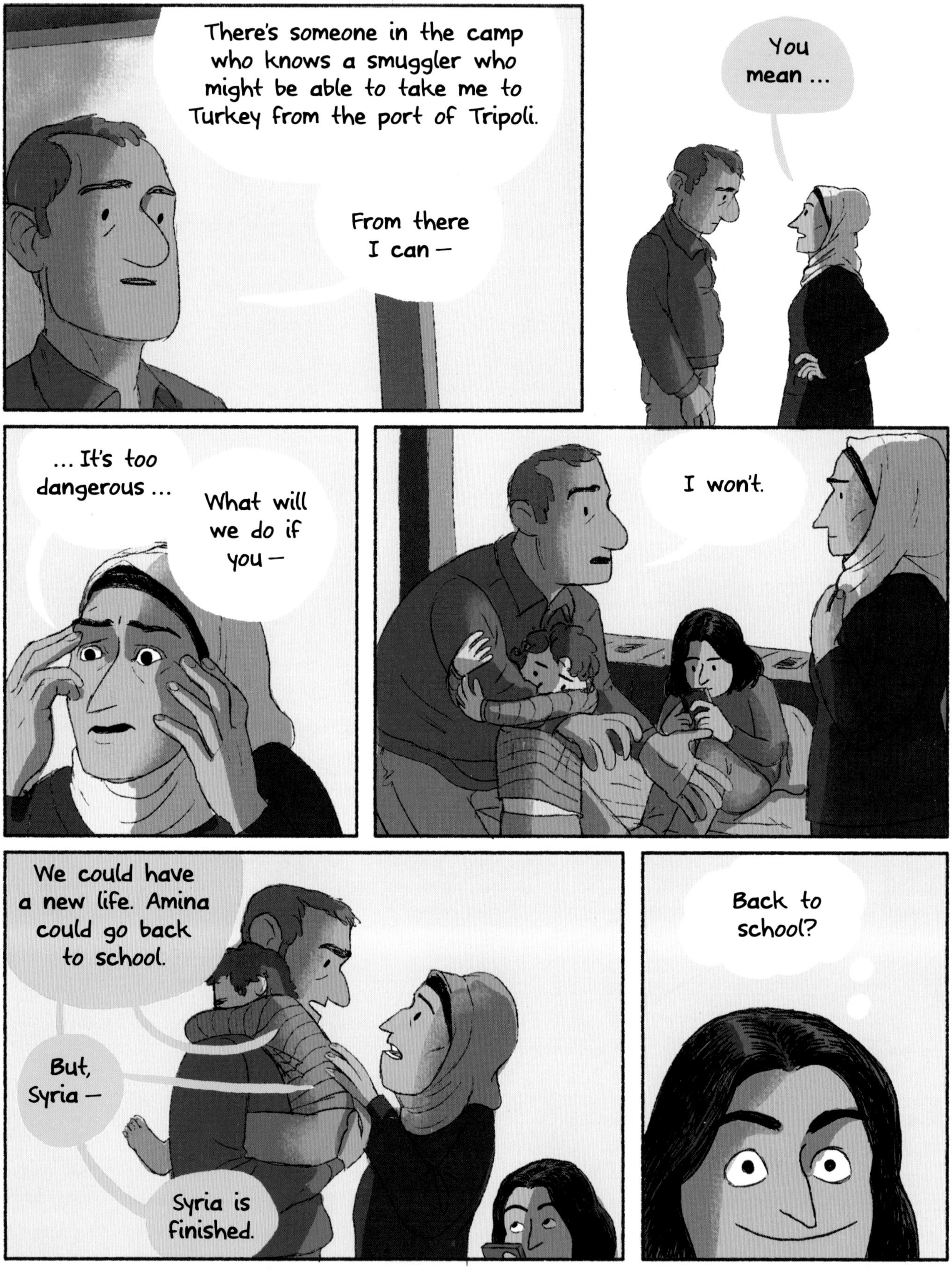
There's someone in the camp who knows a smuggler who might be able to take me to Turkey from the port of Tripoli.
From there I can —
You mean ...
... It's too dangerous ...
What will we do if you —
I won't.
We could have a new life. Amina could go back to school.
But, Syria —
Syria is finished.
Back to school?

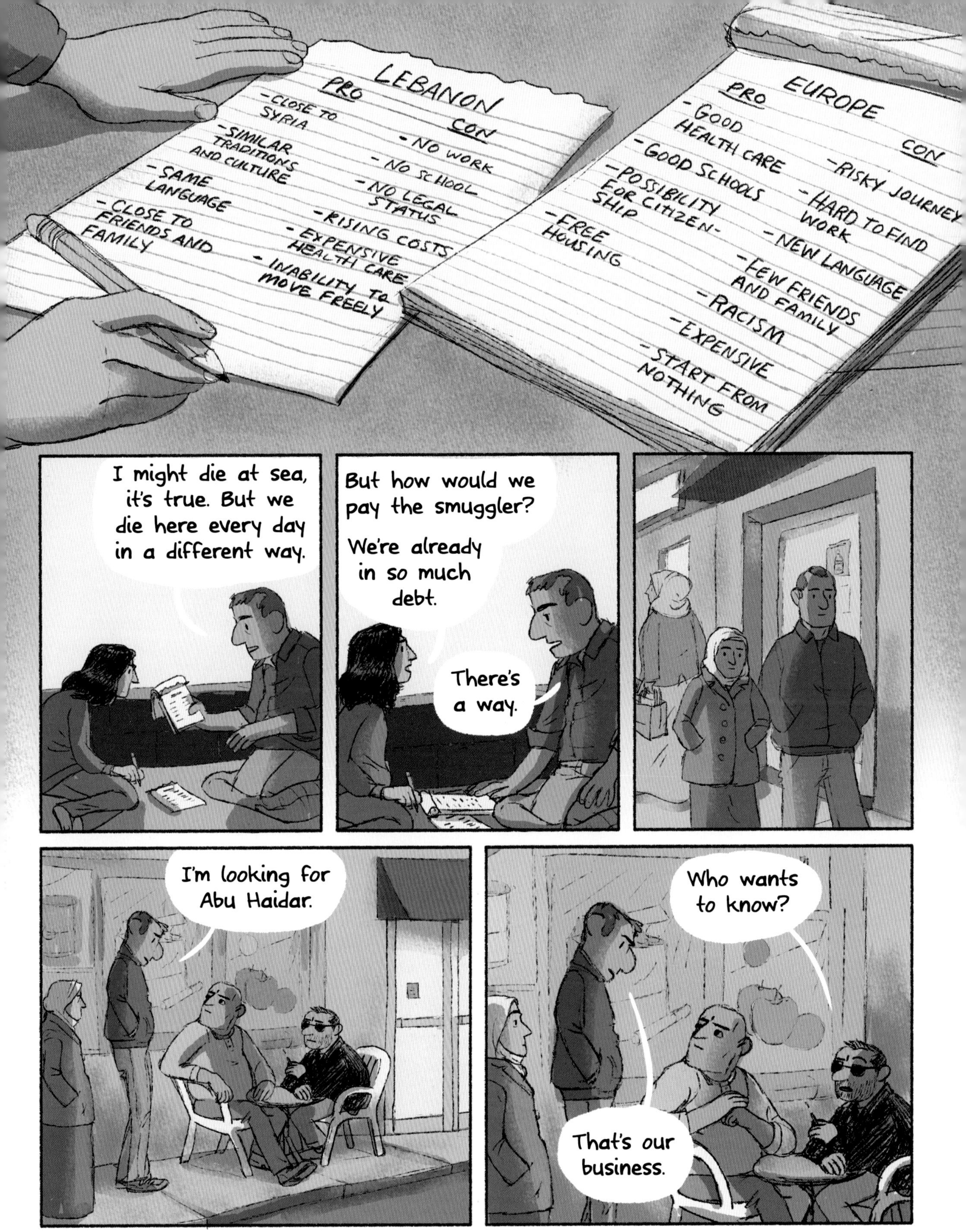
LEBANON
PRO
-CLOSE TO SYRIA
-SIMILAR TRADITIONS AND CULTURE
-SAME LANGUAGE
-CLOSE TO FRIENDS AND FAMILY
CON
-NO WORK
-NO SCHOOL
-NO LEGAL STATUS
-RISING COSTS
-EXPENSIVE HEALTH CARE
-INABILITY TO MOVE FREELY
EUROPE
PRO
-GOOD HEALTH CARE
-GOOD SCHOOLS
-POSSIBILITY FOR CITIZEN-SHIP
-FREE HOUSING
CON
-RISKY JOURNEY
-HARD TO FIND WORK
-NEW LANGUAGE
-FEW FRIENDS AND FAMILY
-RACISM
-EXPENSIVE
-START FROM NOTHING
I might die at sea, it's true. But we die here every day in a different way.
But how would we pay the smuggler?
We're already in so much debt.
There's a way.
I'm looking for Abu Haidar.
Who wants to know?
That's our business.

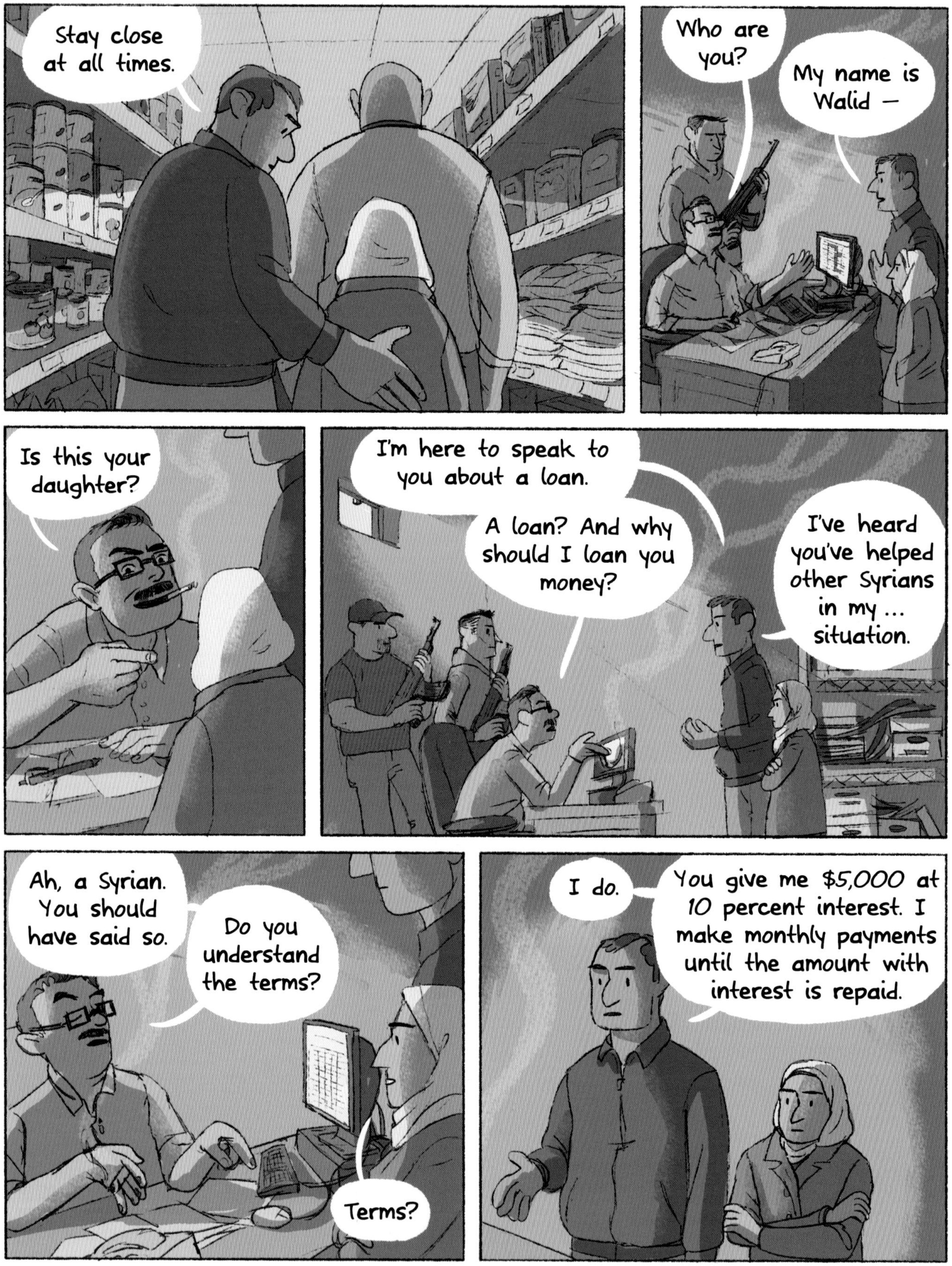
Stay close at all times.
Who are you?
My name is Walid —
Is this your daughter?
I'm here to speak to you about a loan.
A loan? And why should I loan you money?
I've heard you've helped other Syrians in my ... situation.
Ah, a Syrian. You should have said so.
Do you understand the terms?
Terms?
I do.
You give me $5,000 at 10 percent interest. I make monthly payments until the amount with interest is repaid.

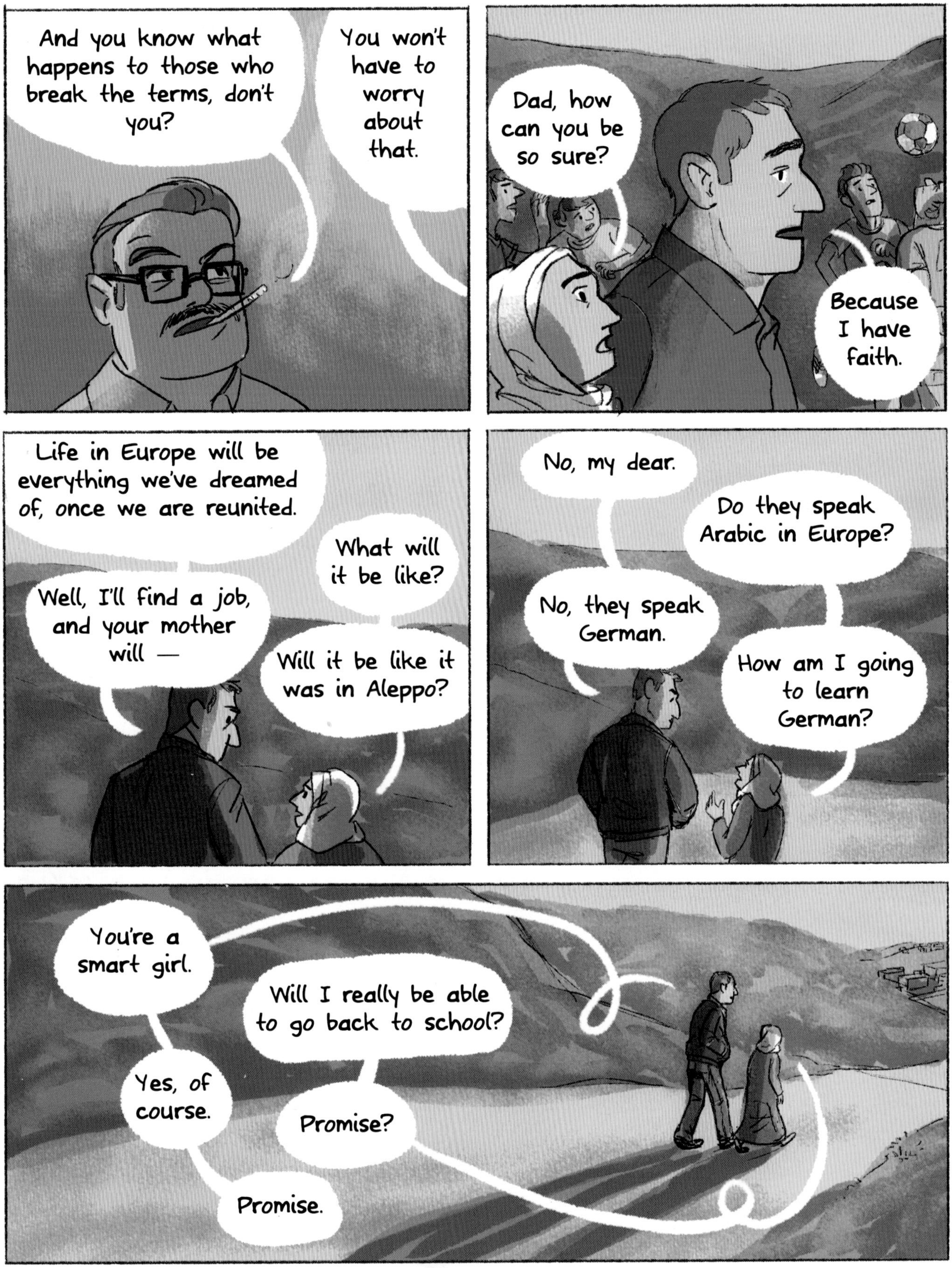
And you know what happens to those who break the terms, don't you?
You won't have to worry about that.
Dad, how can you be so sure?
Because I have faith.
Life in Europe will be everything we've dreamed of, once we are reunited.
What will it be like?
Well, I'll find a job, and your mother will —
Will it be like it was in Aleppo?
No, my dear.
Do they speak Arabic in Europe?
No, they speak German.
How am I going to learn German?
You're a smart girl.
Will I really be able to go back to school?
Yes, of course.
Promise?
Promise.

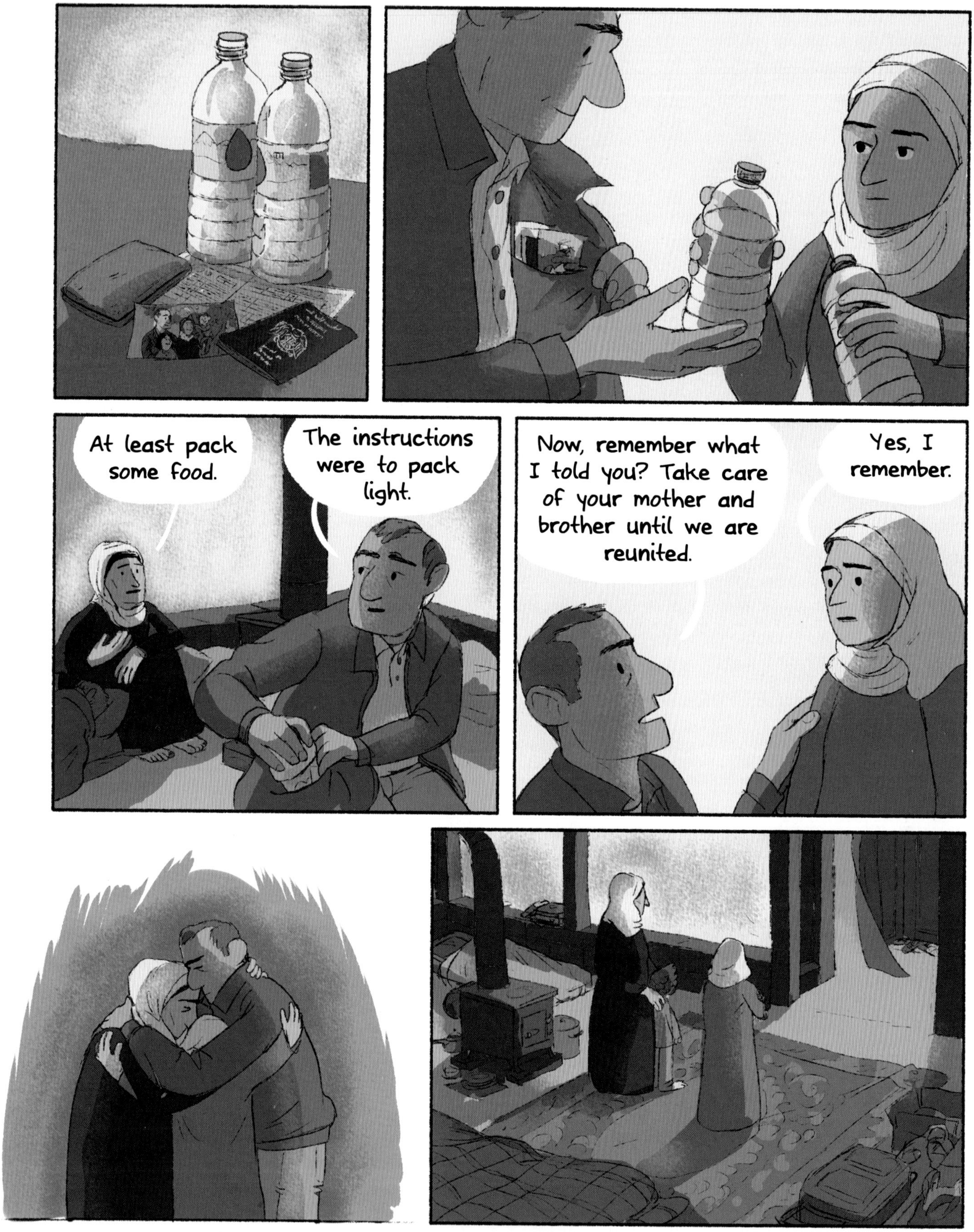
At least pack some food.
The instructions were to pack light.
Now, remember what I told you? Take care of your mother and brother until we are reunited.
Yes, I remember.

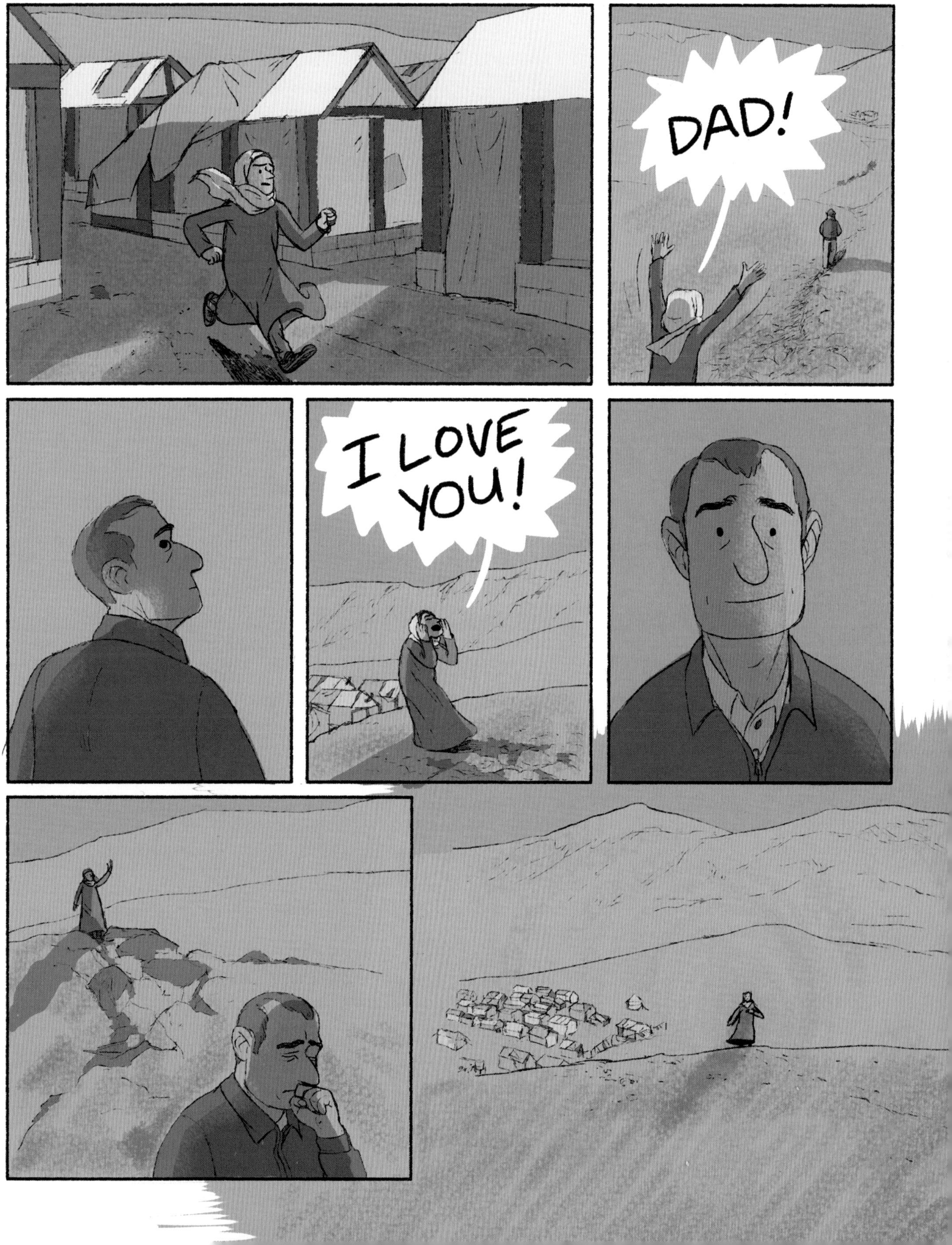
DAD!
I LOVE YOU!

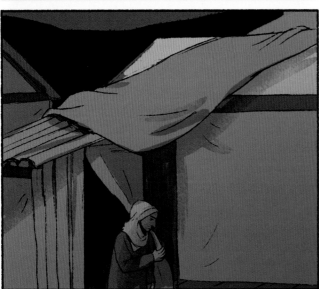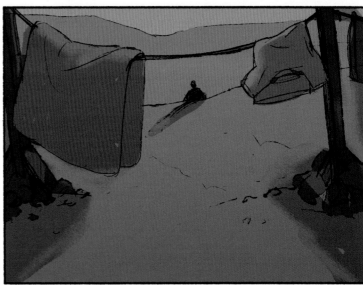

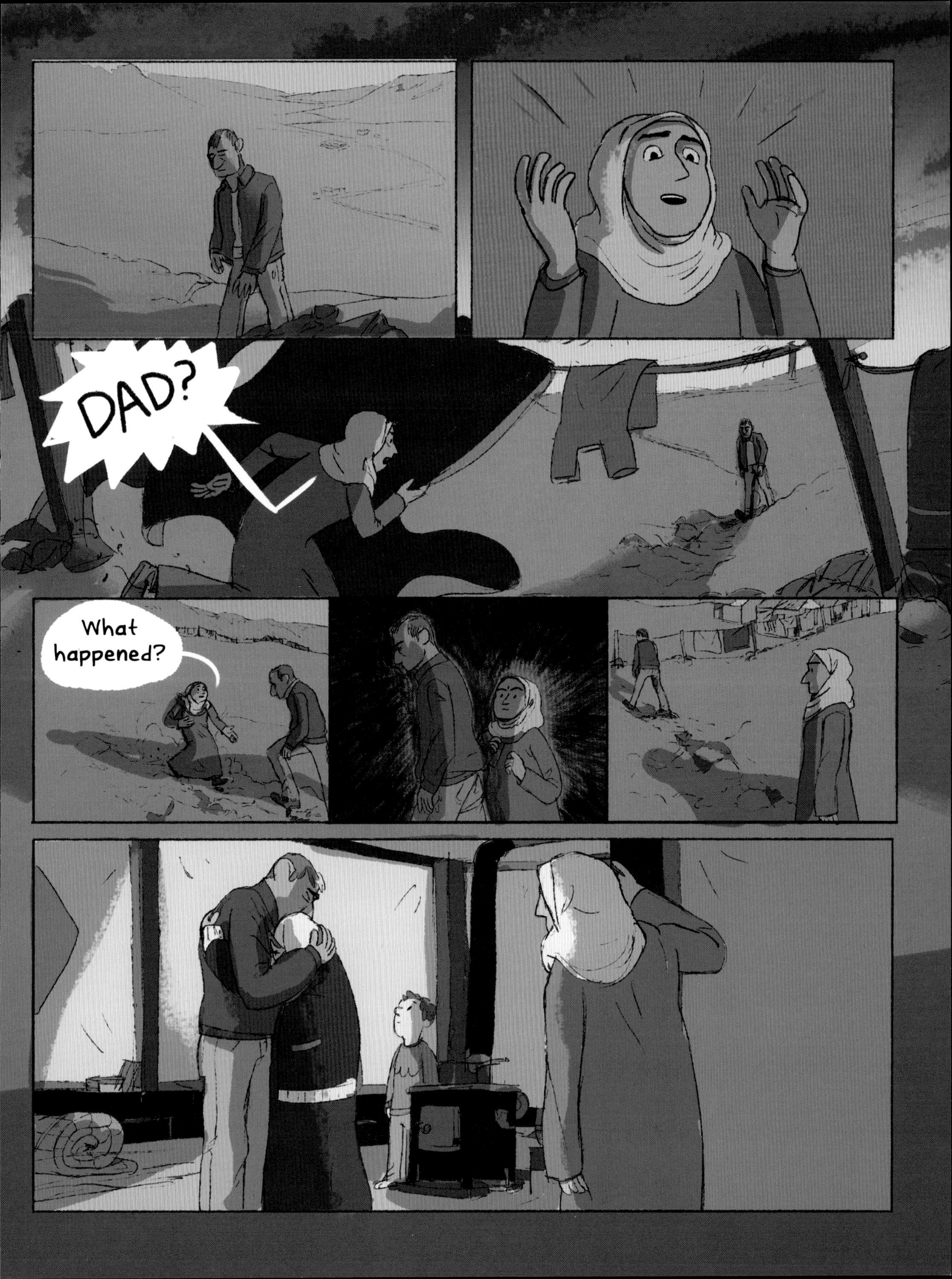
DAD?
What happened?

The smugglers are monsters.

I can't do it!

Get in! Or we will kill you, right here!

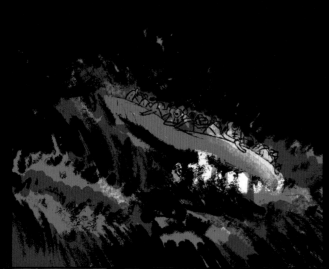

WEE-OO

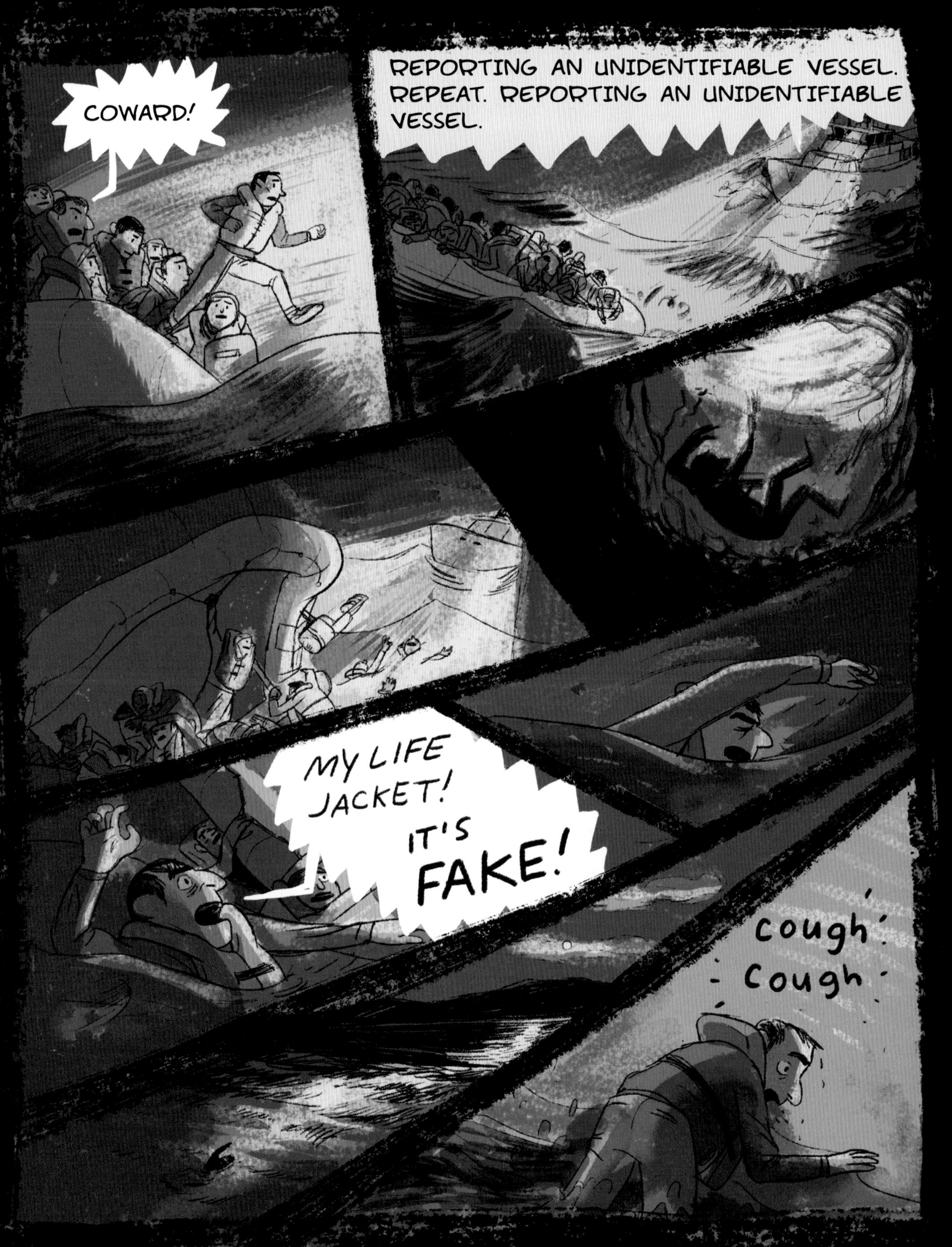
COWARD!
REPORTING AN UNIDENTIFIABLE VESSEL. REPEAT. REPORTING AN UNIDENTIFIABLE VESSEL.
MY LIFE JACKET! IT'S FAKE!
cough cough

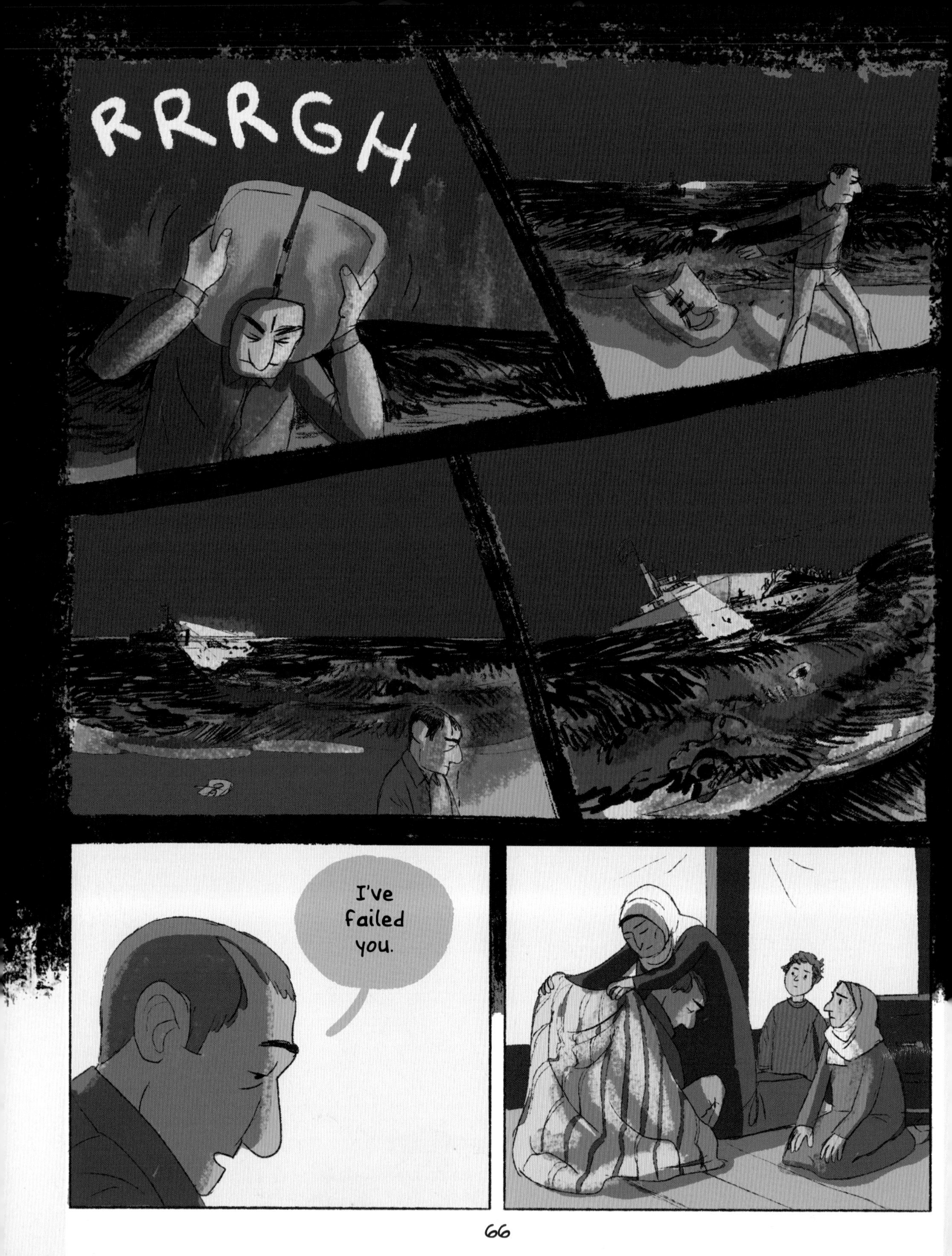
RRRGH
I've failed you.

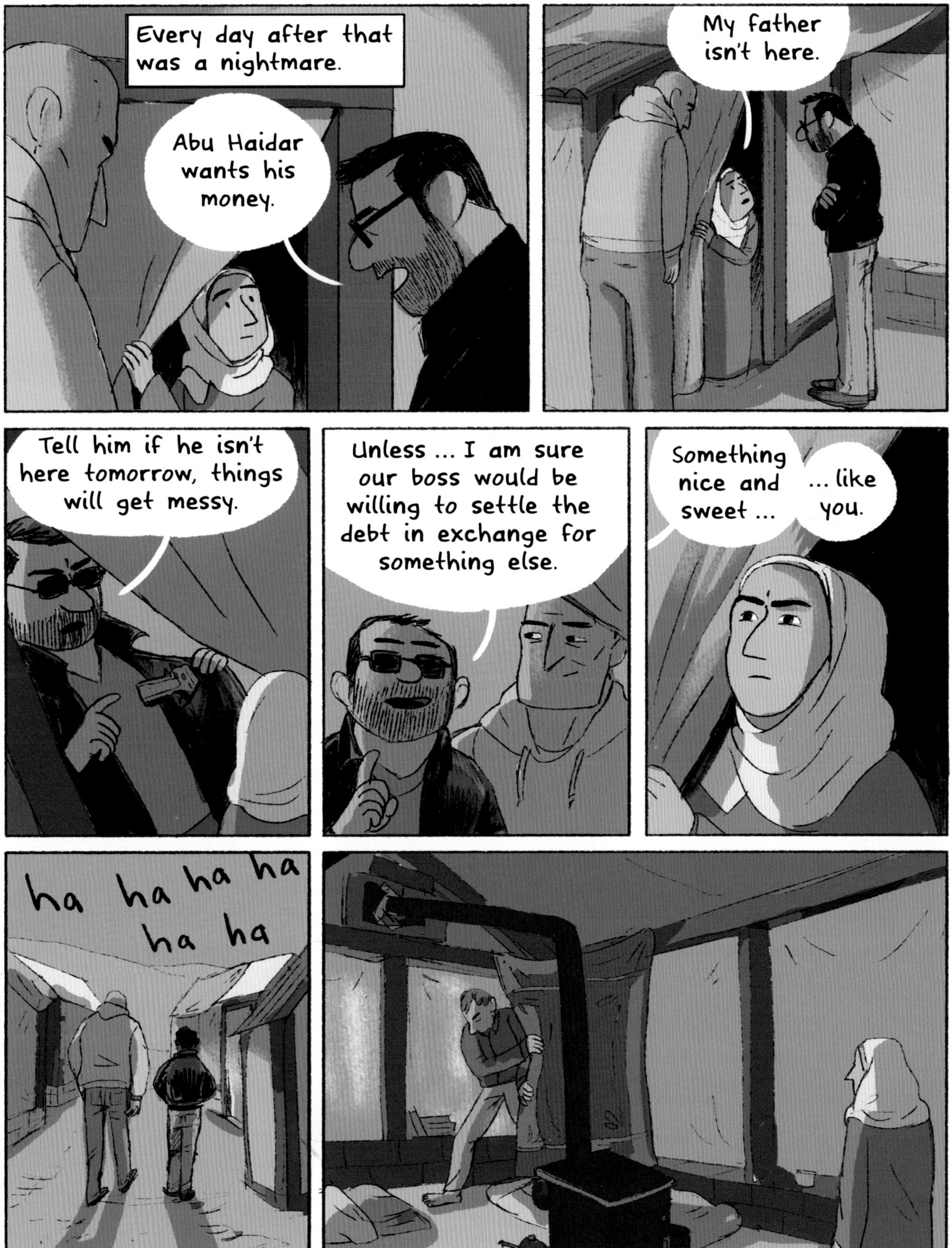
Every day after that was a nightmare.
Abu Haidar wants his money.
My father isn't here.
Tell him if he isn't here tomorrow, things will get messy.
Unless ... I am sure our boss would be willing to settle the debt in exchange for something else.
Something nice and sweet ...
... like you.
ha ha ha ha
ha ha

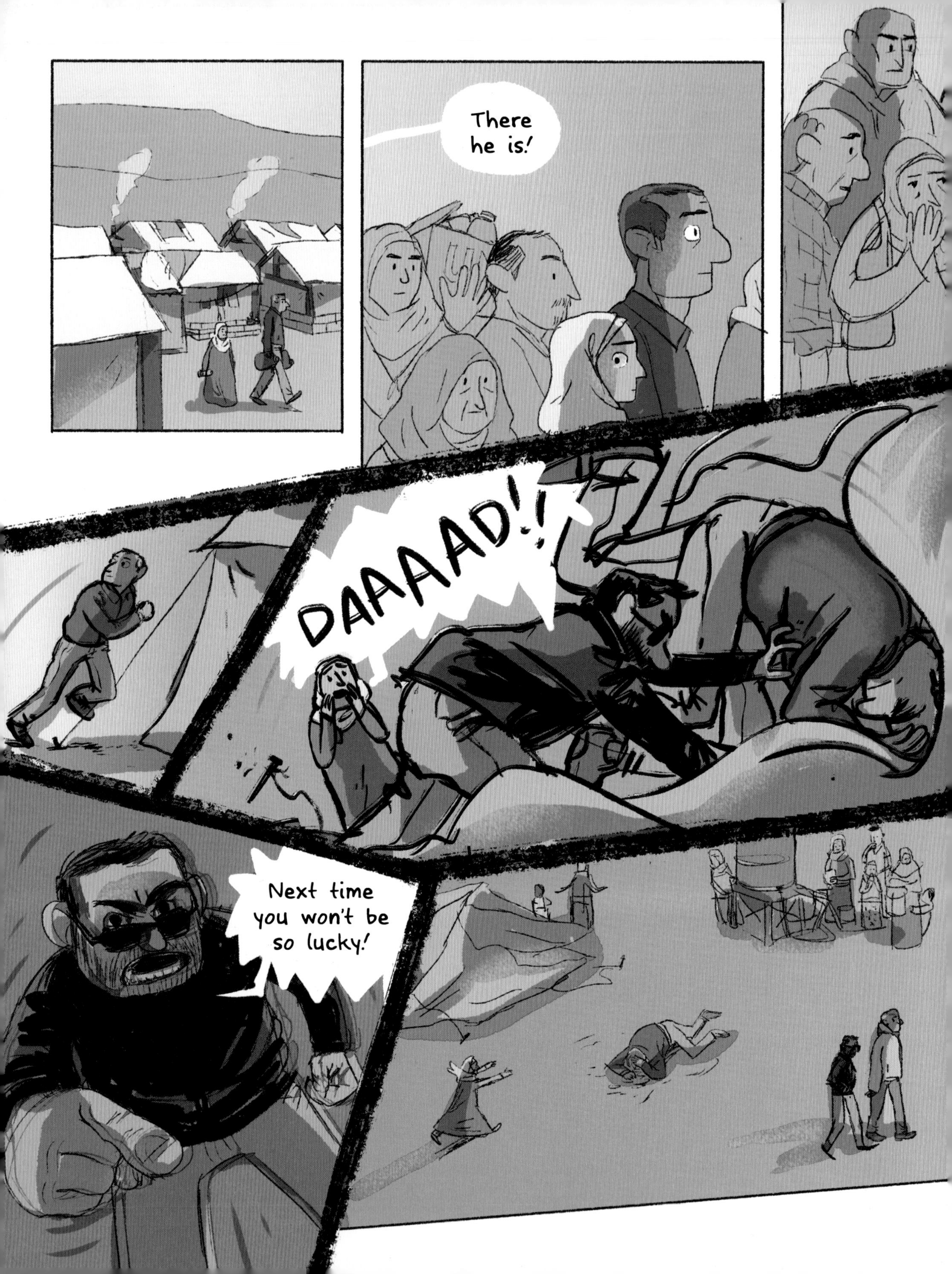
There he is!
DAAAAD!!
Next time you won't be so lucky!

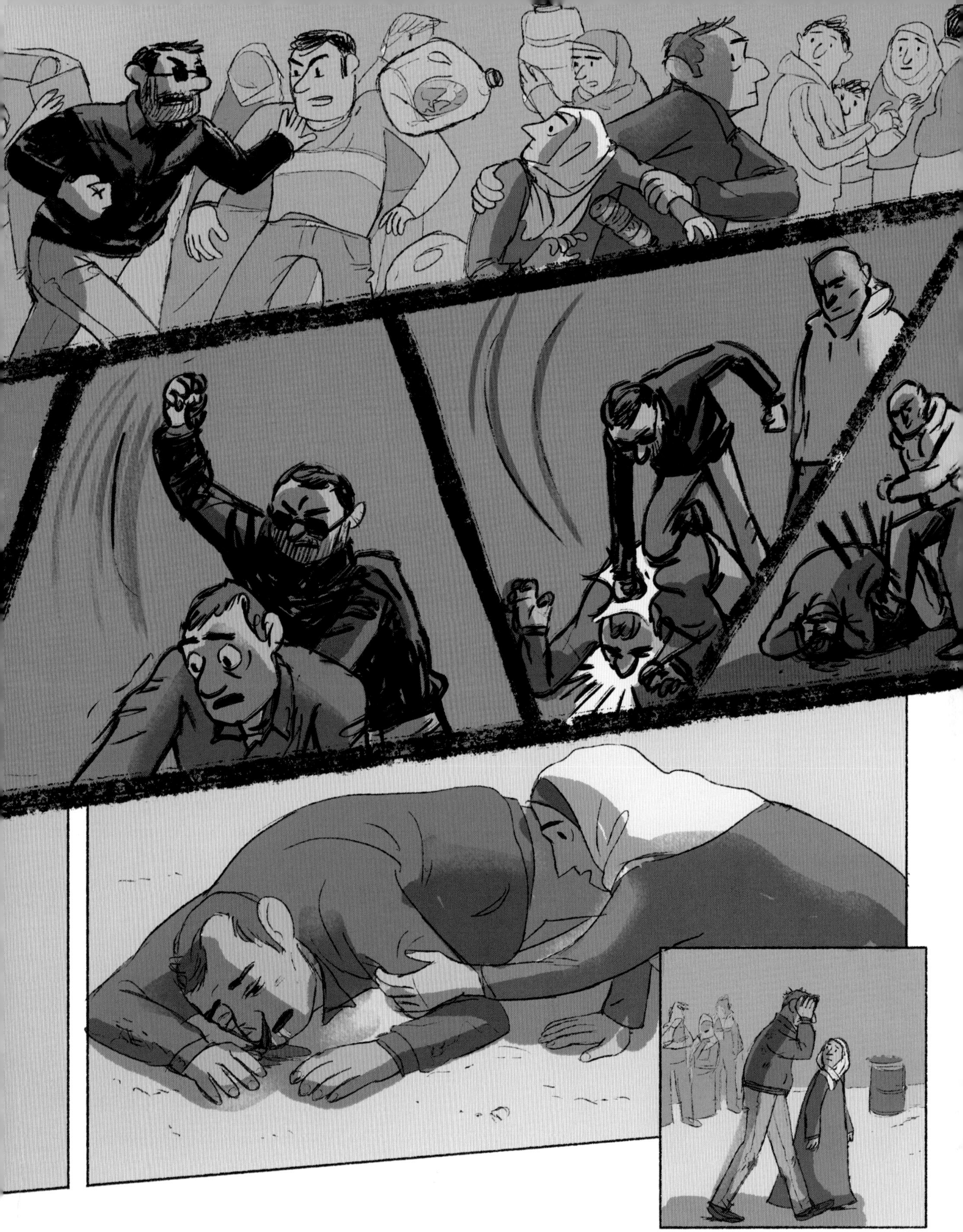

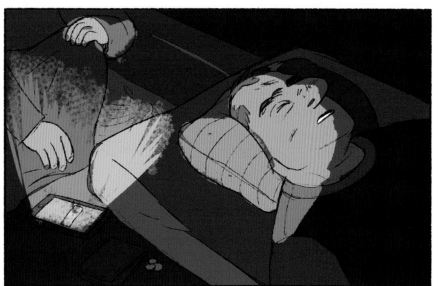

Walid, the government troops blocked the only road out of town!

We're preparing for a siege.

Eastern rebel-held Aleppo, 2016.

BOOOM

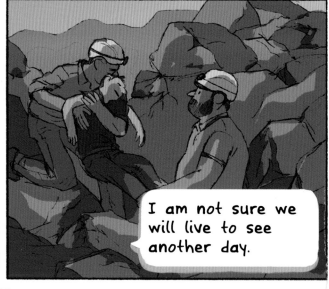

I am not sure we will live to see another day.

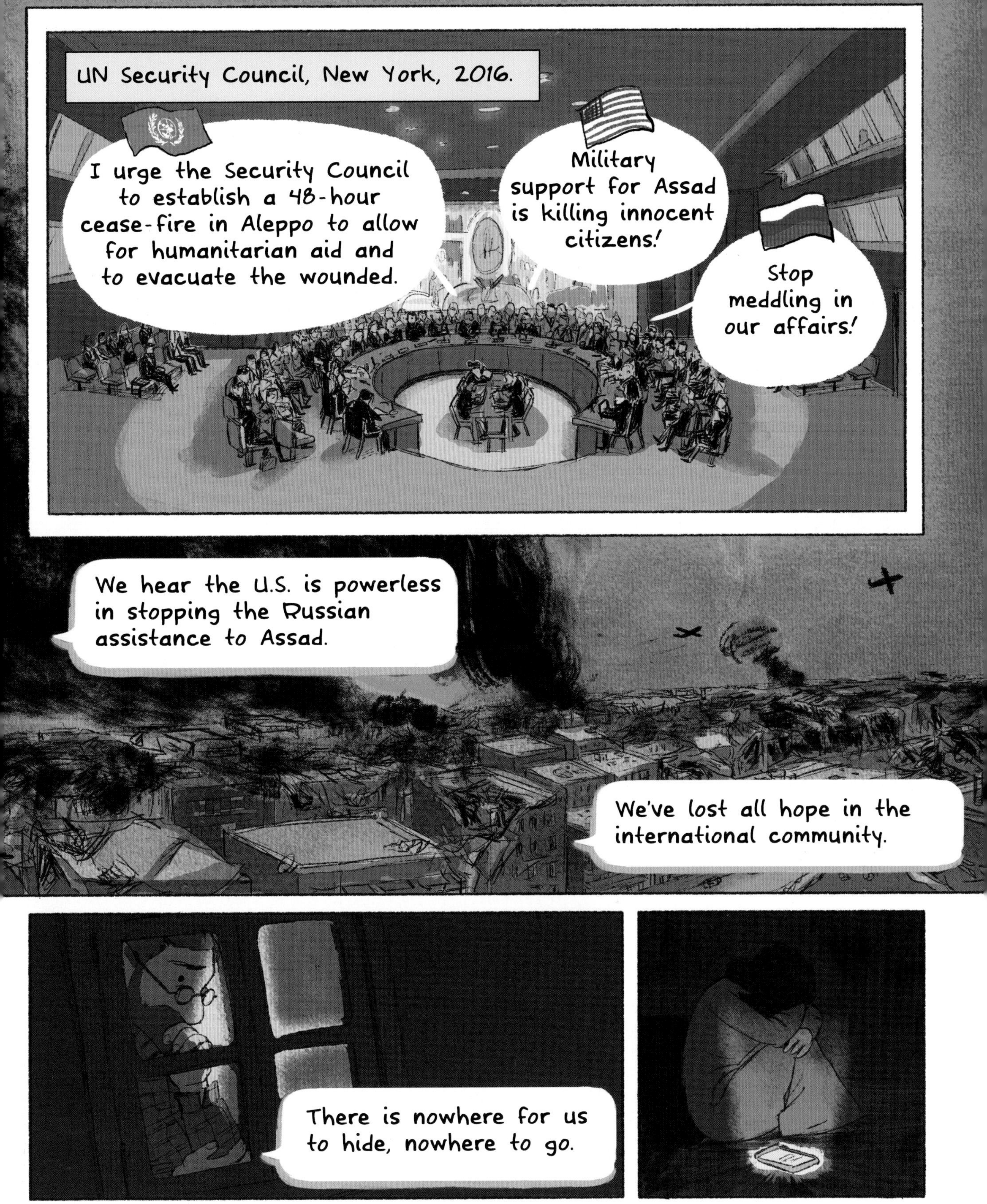
UN Security Council, New York, 2016.
I urge the Security Council to establish a 48-hour cease-fire in Aleppo to allow for humanitarian aid and to evacuate the wounded.
Military support for Assad is killing innocent citizens!
Stop meddling in our affairs!
We hear the U.S. is powerless in stopping the Russian assistance to Assad.
We've lost all hope in the international community.
There is nowhere for us to hide, nowhere to go.

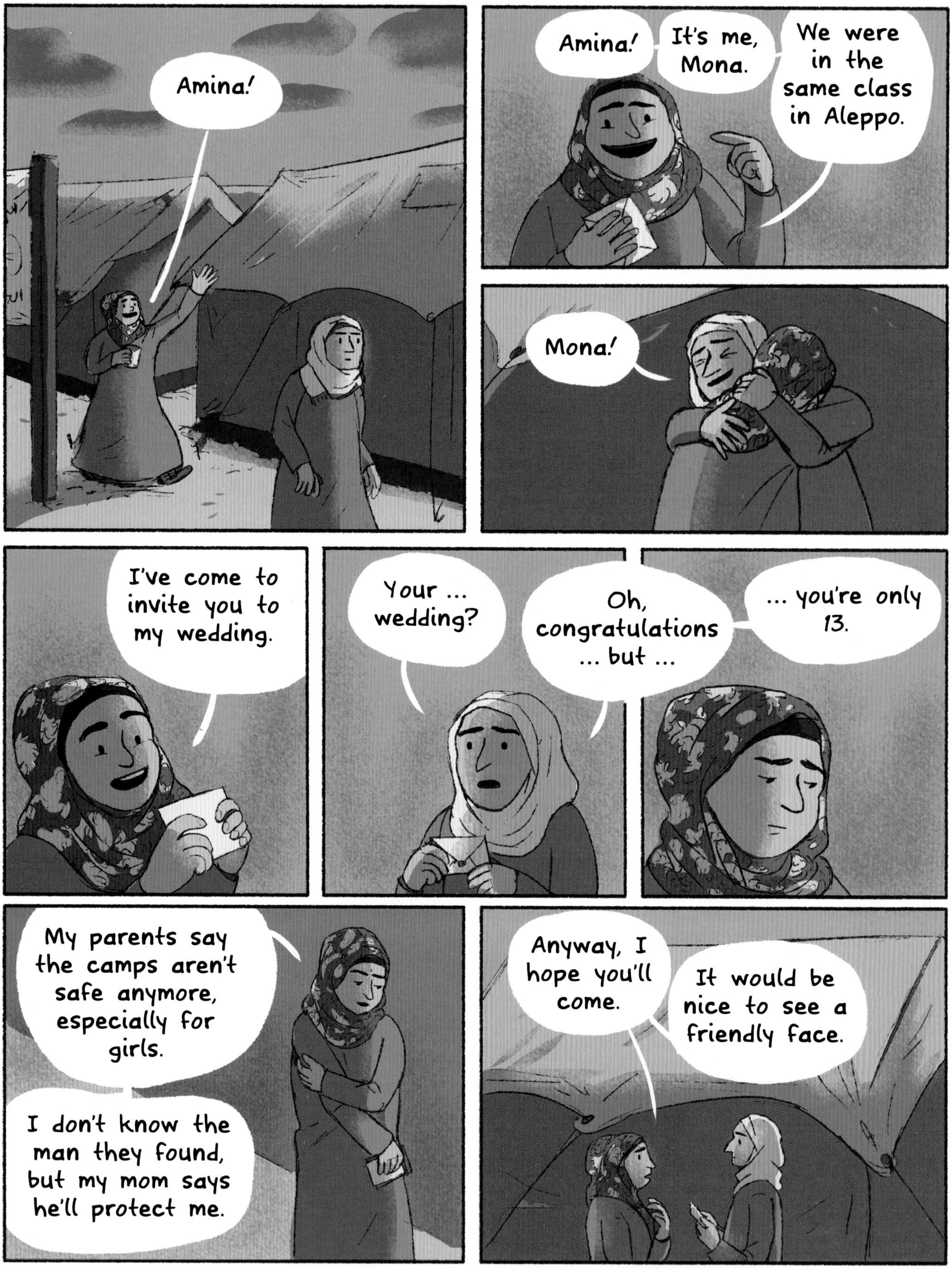
Amina!
Amina!
It's me, Mona.
We were in the same class in Aleppo.
Mona!
I've come to invite you to my wedding.
Your ... wedding?
Oh, congratulations ... but ...
... you're only 13.
My parents say the camps aren't safe anymore, especially for girls.
I don't know the man they found, but my mom says he'll protect me.
Anyway, I hope you'll come.
It would be nice to see a friendly face.

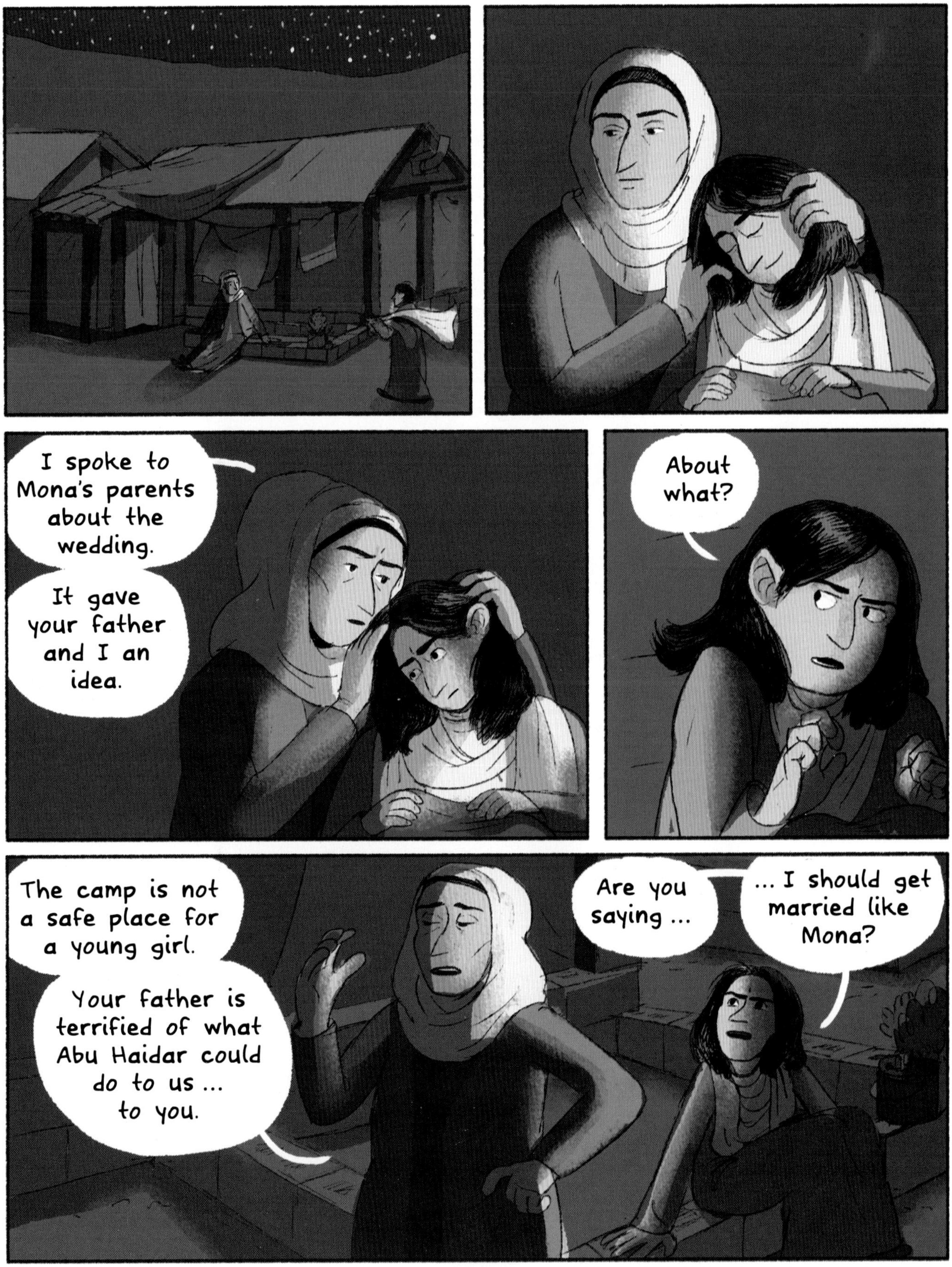
I spoke to Mona's parents about the wedding.
It gave your father and I an idea.
About what?
The camp is not a safe place for a young girl.
Your father is terrified of what Abu Haidar could do to us ... to you.
Are you saying ...
... I should get married like Mona?

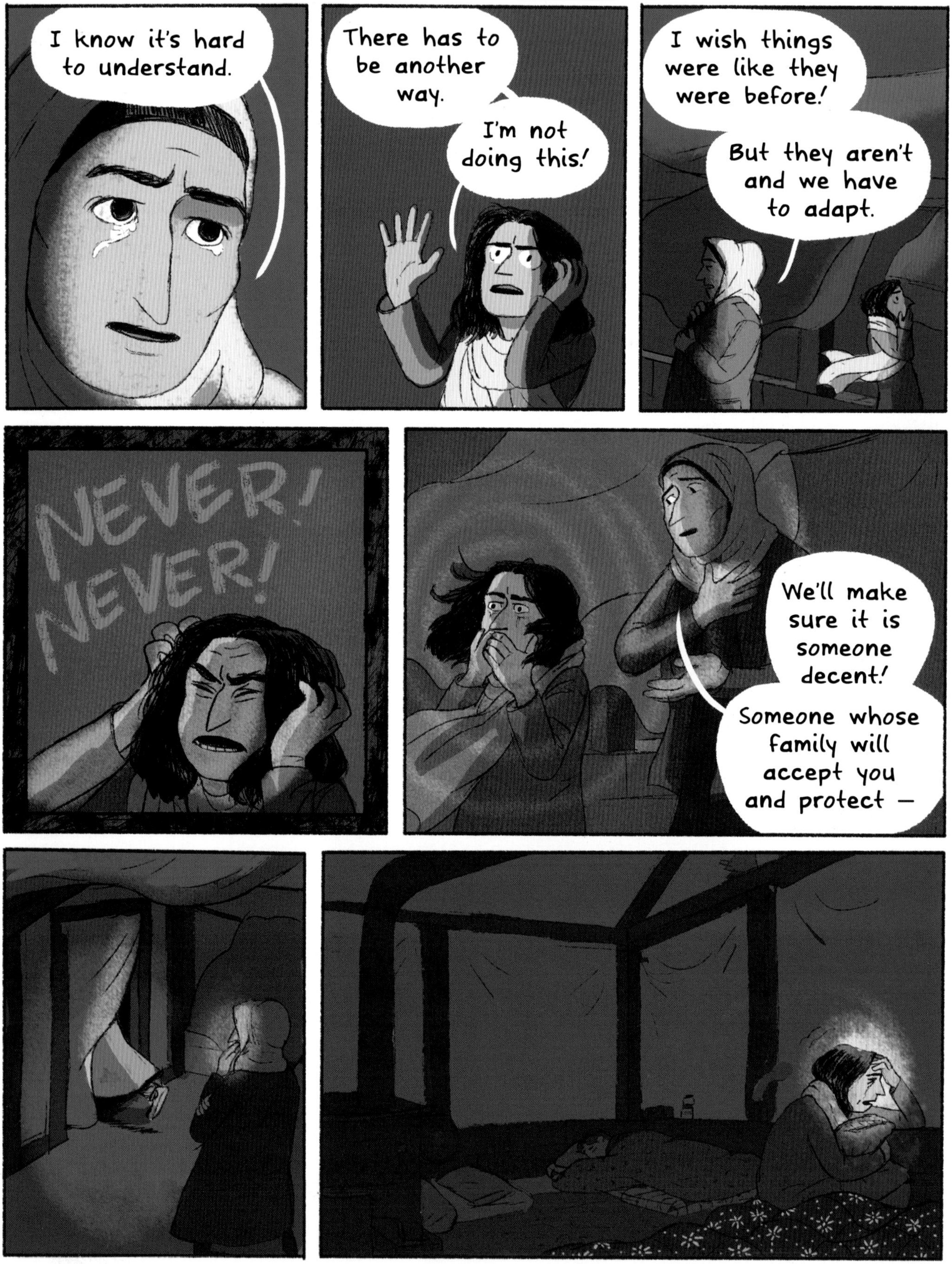
I know it's hard to understand.
There has to be another way.
I'm not doing this!
I wish things were like they were before!
But they aren't and we have to adapt.
NEVER! NEVER!
We'll make sure it is someone decent!
Someone whose family will accept you and protect –

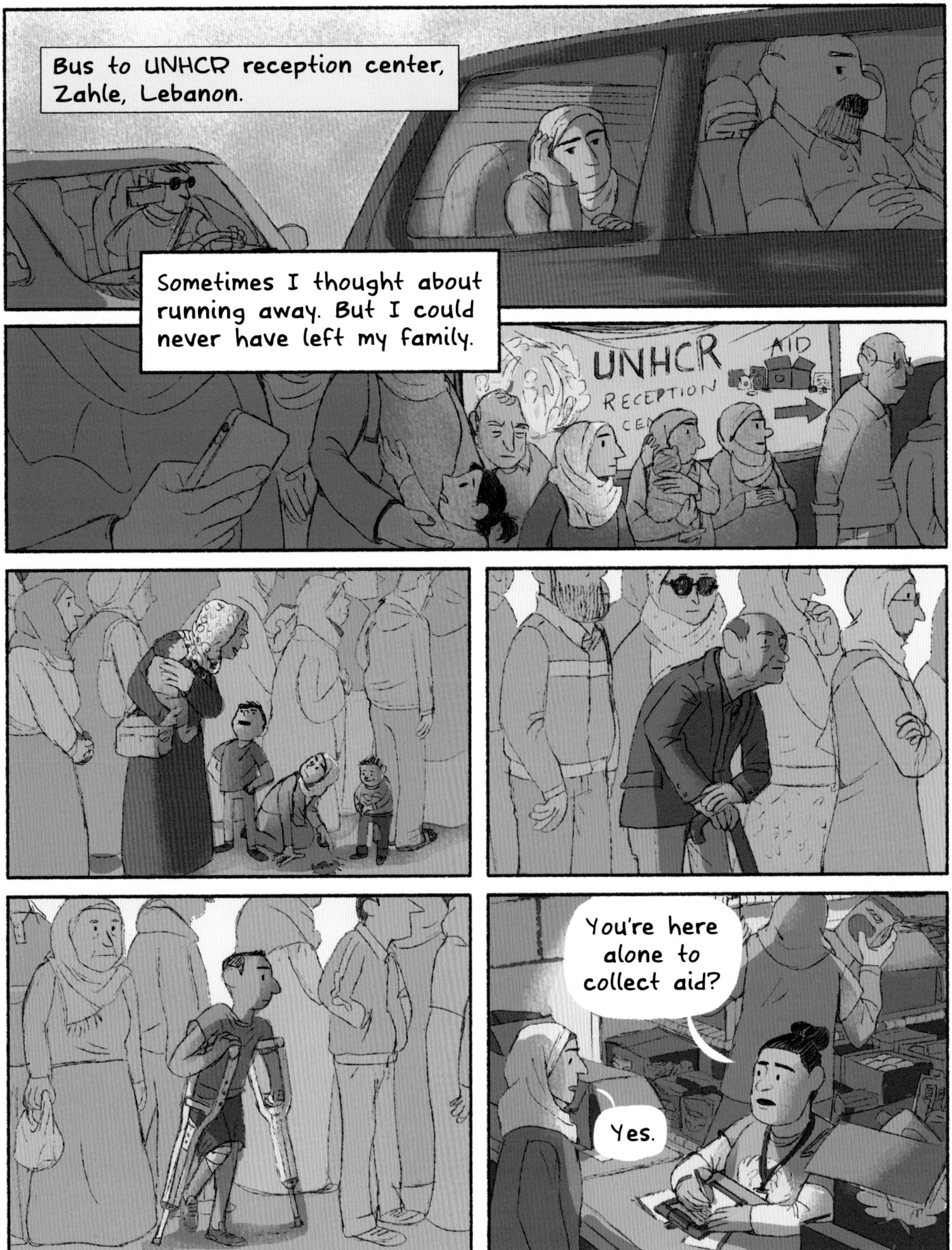
Bus to UNHCR reception center, Zahle, Lebanon.
Sometimes I thought about running away. But I could never have left my family.
UNHCR
AID
RECEPTION
You're here alone to collect aid?
Yes.

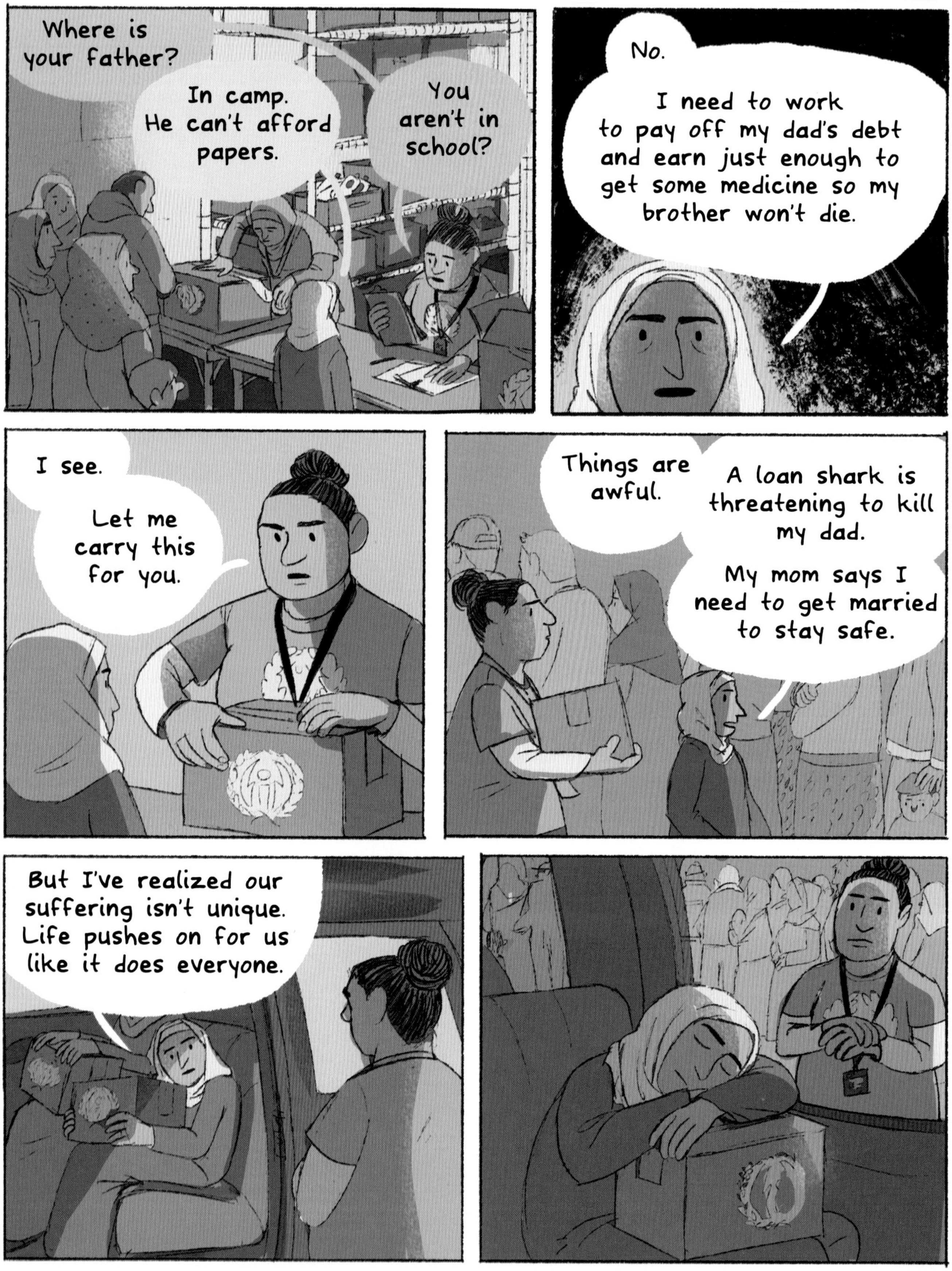
Where is your father?
In camp. He can't afford papers.
You aren't in school?
No.
I need to work to pay off my dad's debt and earn just enough to get some medicine so my brother won't die.
I see.
Let me carry this for you.
Things are awful.
A loan shark is threatening to kill my dad.
My mom says I need to get married to stay safe.
But I've realized our suffering isn't unique. Life pushes on for us like it does everyone.

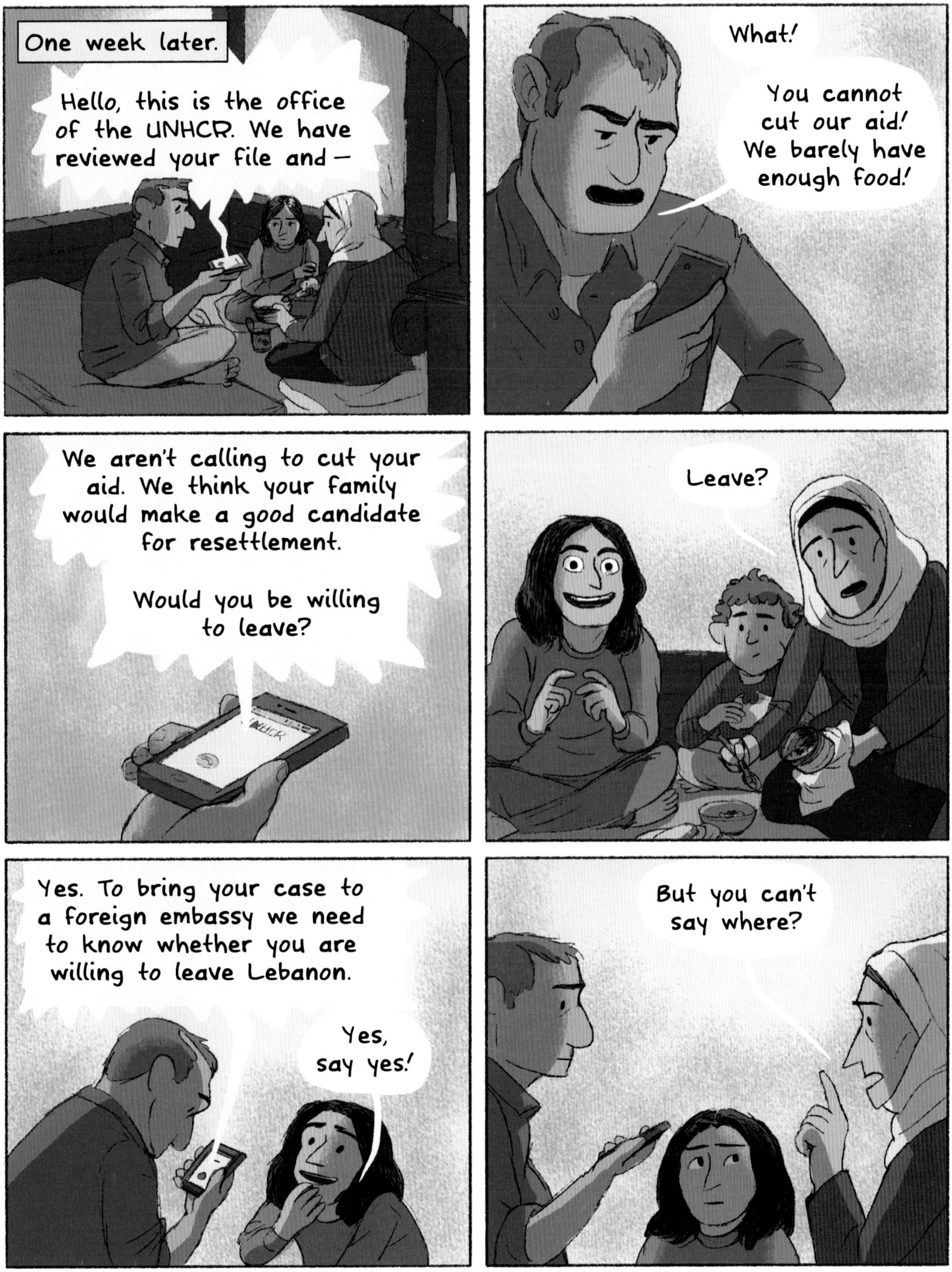
One week later.
Hello, this is the office of the UNHCR. We have reviewed your file and —
What!
You cannot cut our aid! We barely have enough food!
We aren't calling to cut your aid. We think your family would make a good candidate for resettlement.
Would you be willing to leave?
UNHCR
Leave?
Yes. To bring your case to a foreign embassy we need to know whether you are willing to leave Lebanon.
Yes, say yes!
But you can't say where?

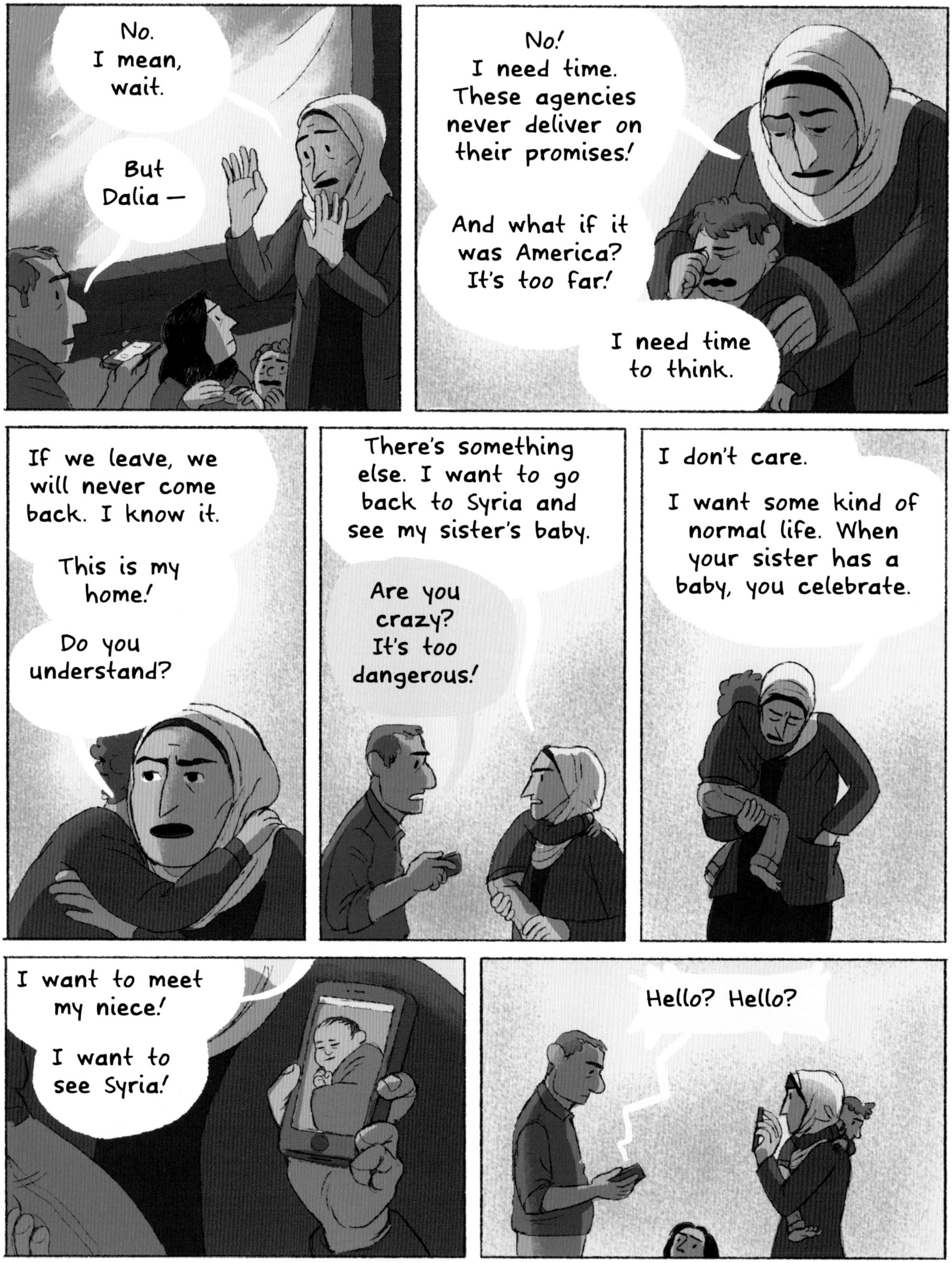
No. I mean, wait.
But Dalia —
No! I need time. These agencies never deliver on their promises!
And what if it was America? It's too far!
I need time to think.
If we leave, we will never come back. I know it.
This is my home!
Do you understand?
There's something else. I want to go back to Syria and see my sister's baby.
Are you crazy? It's too dangerous!
I don't care.
I want some kind of normal life. When your sister has a baby, you celebrate.
I want to meet my niece!
I want to see Syria!
Hello? Hello?

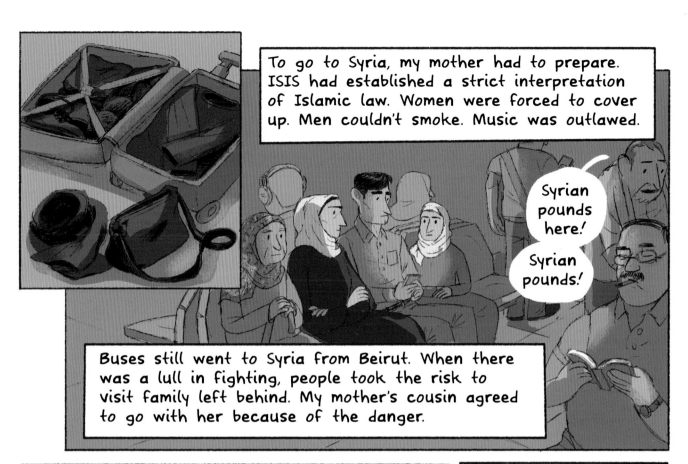

To go to Syria, my mother had to prepare. ISIS had established a strict interpretation of Islamic law. Women were forced to cover up. Men couldn't smoke. Music was outlawed.

Syrian pounds here!

Syrian pounds!

Buses still went to Syria from Beirut. When there was a lull in fighting, people took the risk to visit family left behind. My mother's cousin agreed to go with her because of the danger.

Where are you going, sister?

I am going to Raqqa.

Deir Ezzor, to meet my baby niece.

But that's the ISIS capital! Are you sure it's safe?

What do I care? My one son is lost at sea and my other is trapped in a besieged city. I have a daughter left and I want to see her. Syria might be at war, but it's still home.

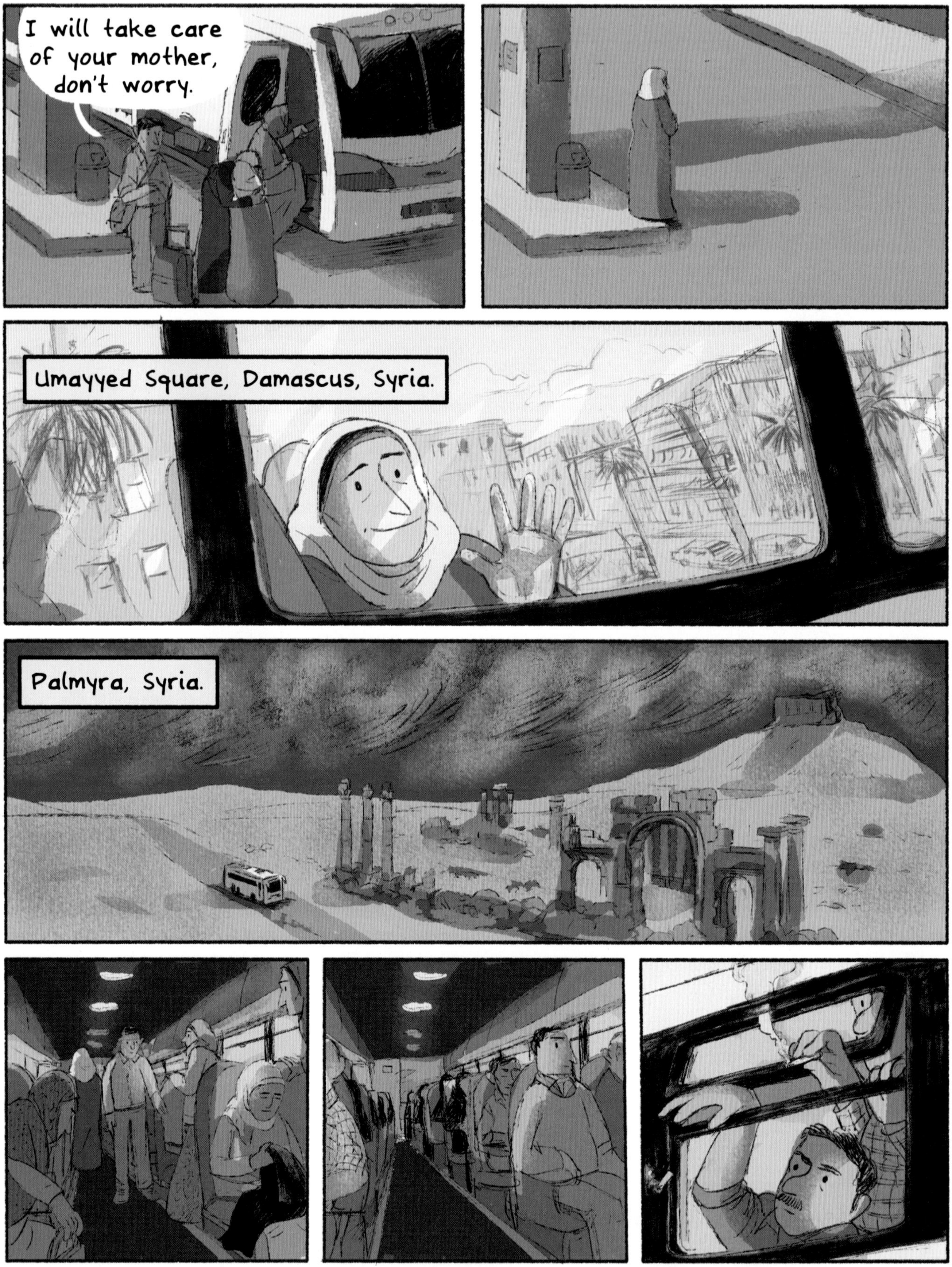
I will take care of your mother, don't worry.
Umayyed Square, Damascus, Syria.
Palmyra, Syria.

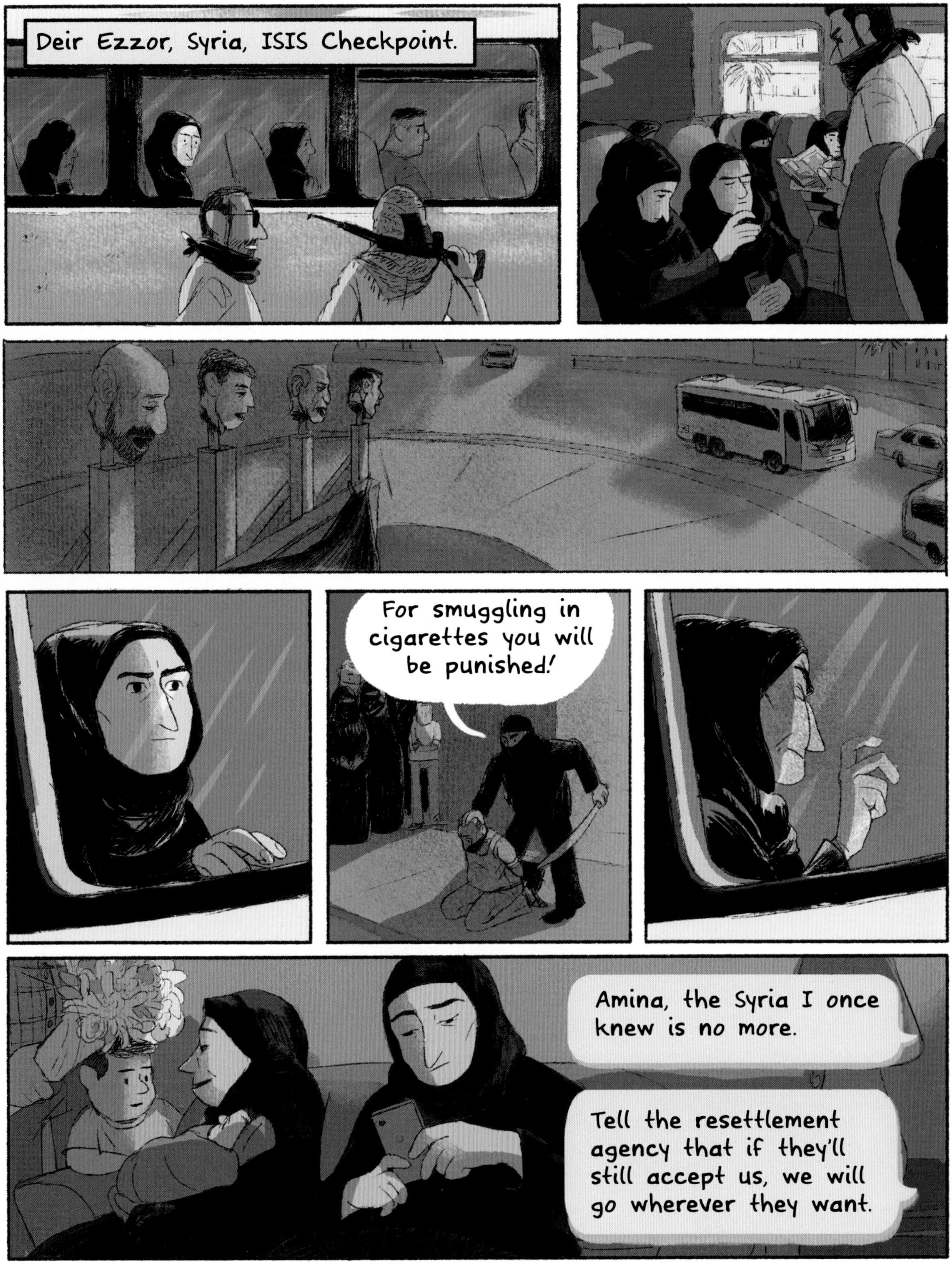
Deir Ezzor, Syria, ISIS Checkpoint.
For smuggling in cigarettes you will be punished!
Amina, the Syria I once knew is no more.
Tell the resettlement agency that if they'll still accept us, we will go wherever they want.

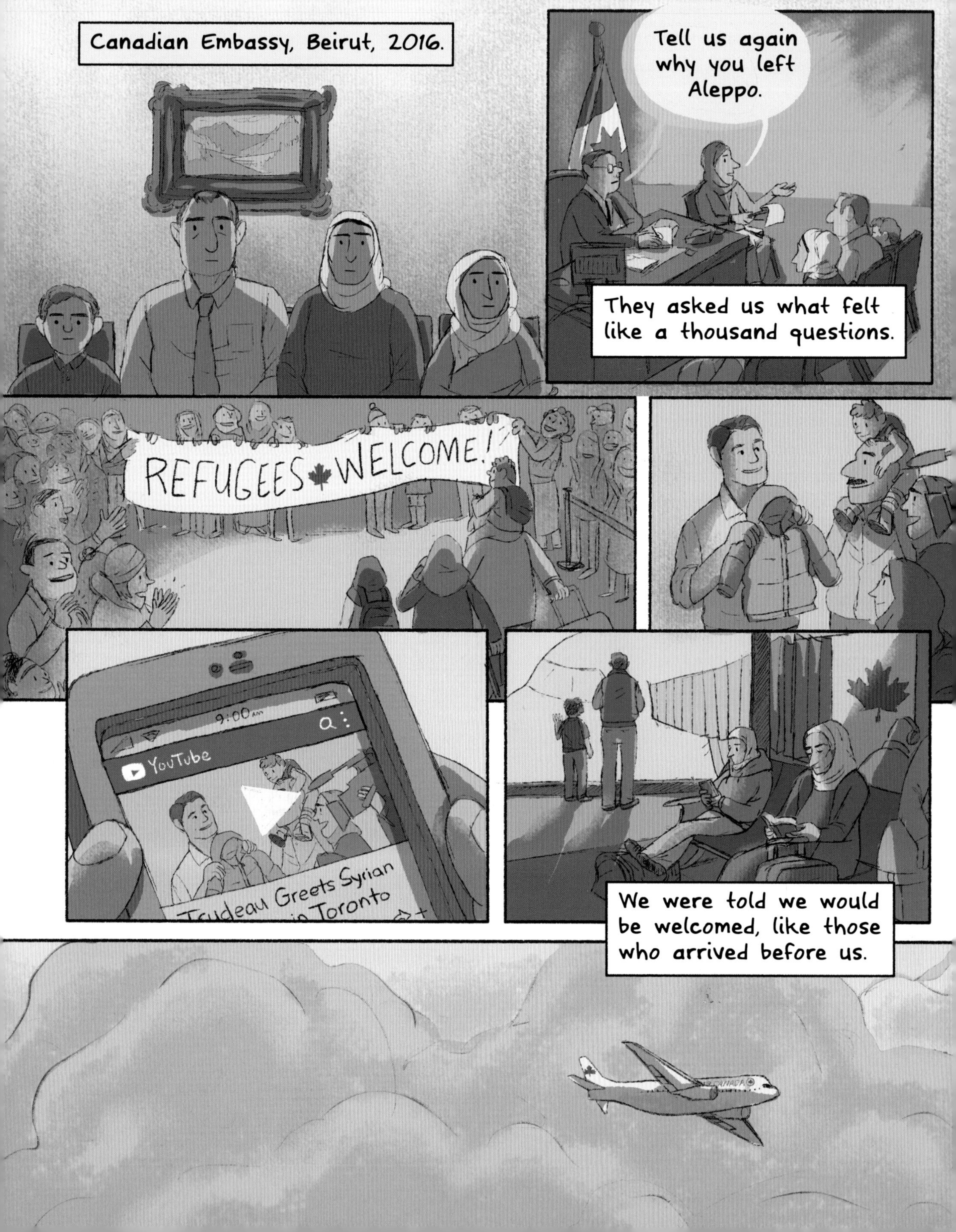
Canadian Embassy, Beirut, 2016.
Tell us again why you left Aleppo.
They asked us what felt like a thousand questions.
REFUGEES WELCOME!
9:00 AM
YouTube
Trudeau Greets Syrian
in Toronto
We were told we would be welcomed, like those who arrived before us.

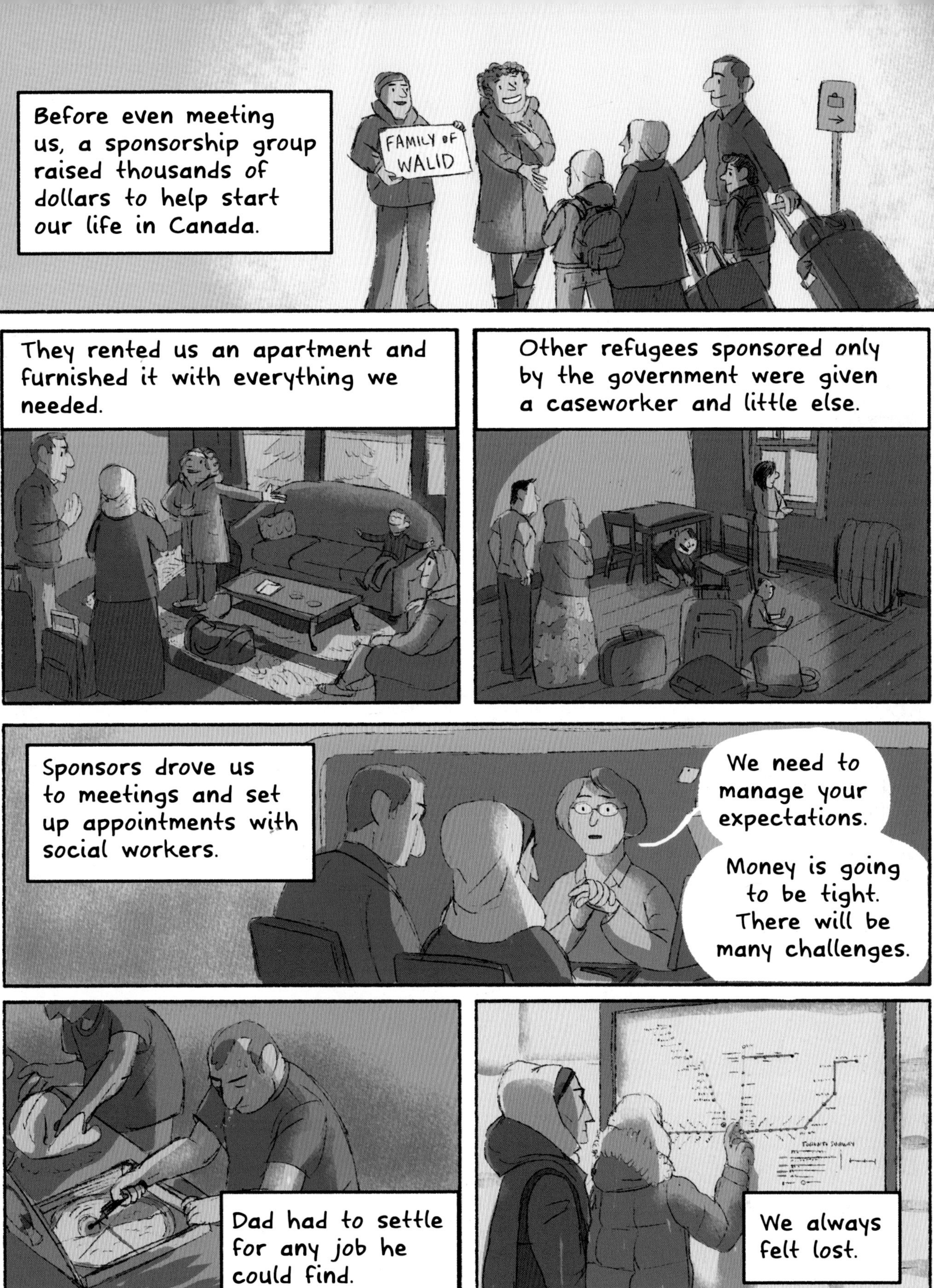
Before even meeting us, a sponsorship group raised thousands of dollars to help start our life in Canada.
FAMILY OF WALID
They rented us an apartment and furnished it with everything we needed.
Other refugees sponsored only by the government were given a caseworker and little else.
Sponsors drove us to meetings and set up appointments with social workers.
We need to manage your expectations.
Money is going to be tight. There will be many challenges.
Dad had to settle for any job he could find.
We always felt lost.

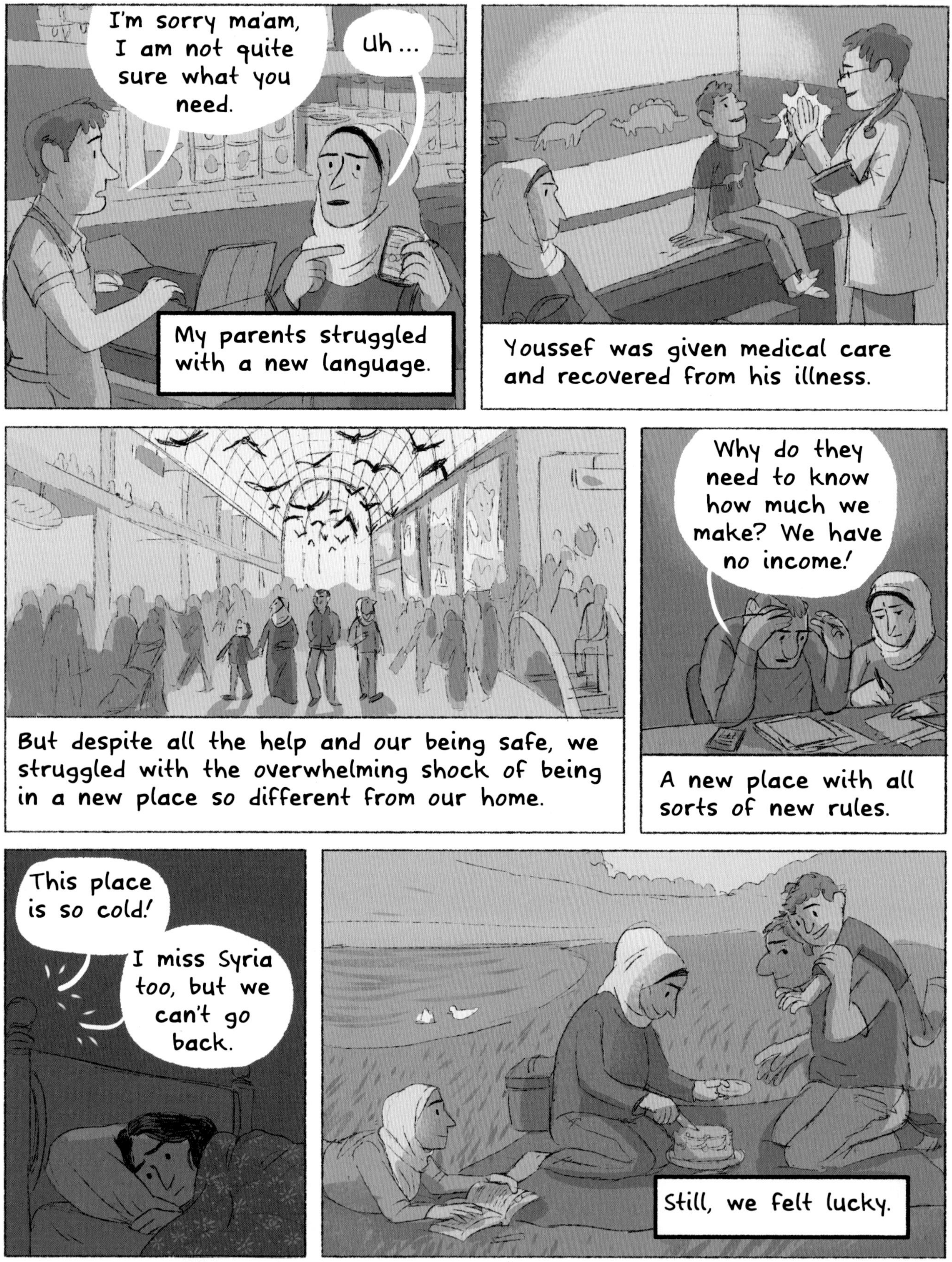
I'm sorry ma'am, I am not quite sure what you need.
Uh ...
My parents struggled with a new language.
Youssef was given medical care and recovered from his illness.
But despite all the help and our being safe, we struggled with the overwhelming shock of being in a new place so different from our home.
Why do they need to know how much we make? We have no income!
A new place with all sorts of new rules.
This place is so cold!
I miss Syria too, but we can't go back.
Still, we felt lucky.

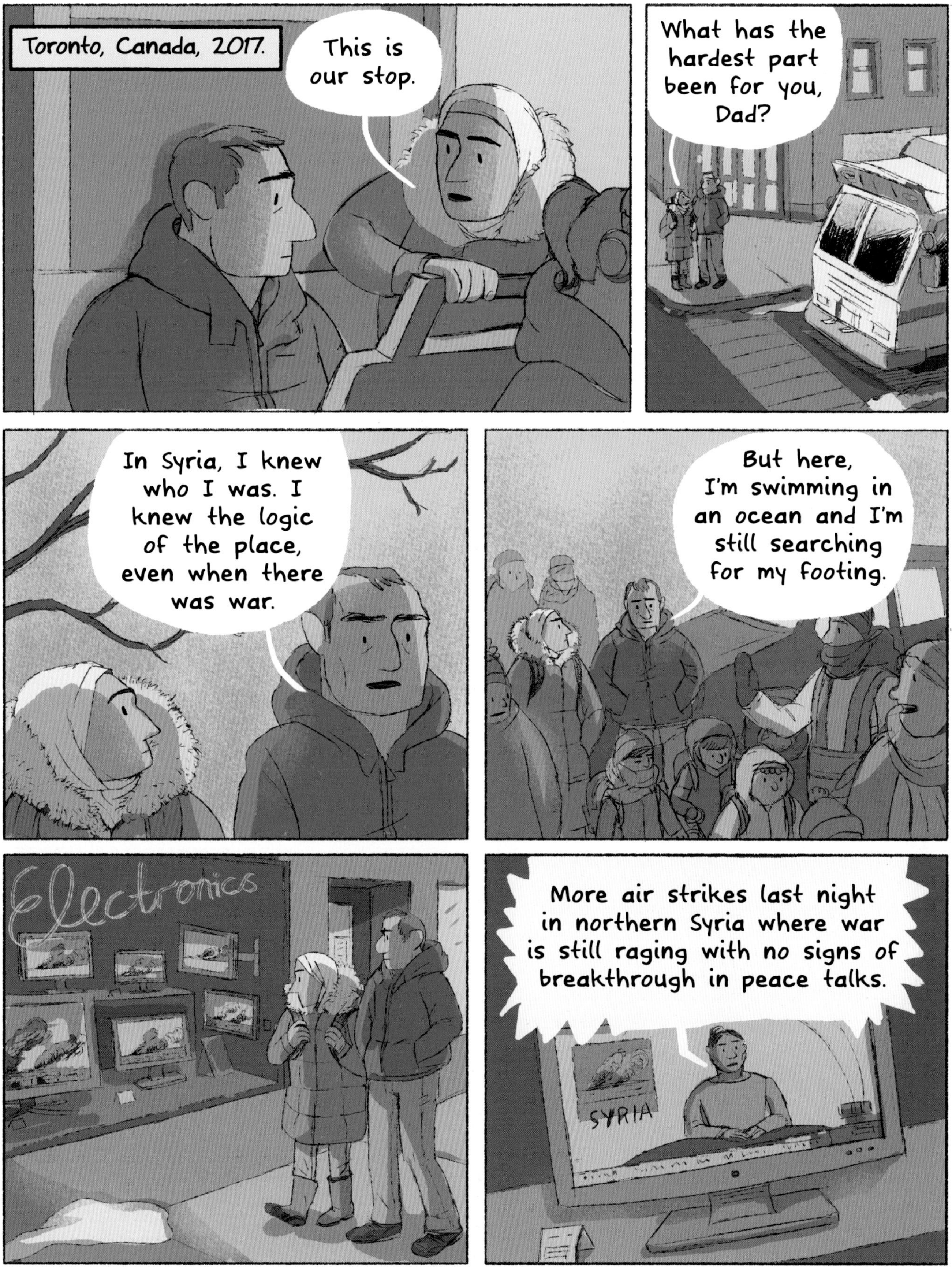
Toronto, Canada, 2017.
This is our stop.
What has the hardest part been for you, Dad?
In Syria, I knew who I was. I knew the logic of the place, even when there was war.
But here, I'm swimming in an ocean and I'm still searching for my footing.
Electronics
More air strikes last night in northern Syria where war is still raging with no signs of breakthrough in peace talks.
SYRIA

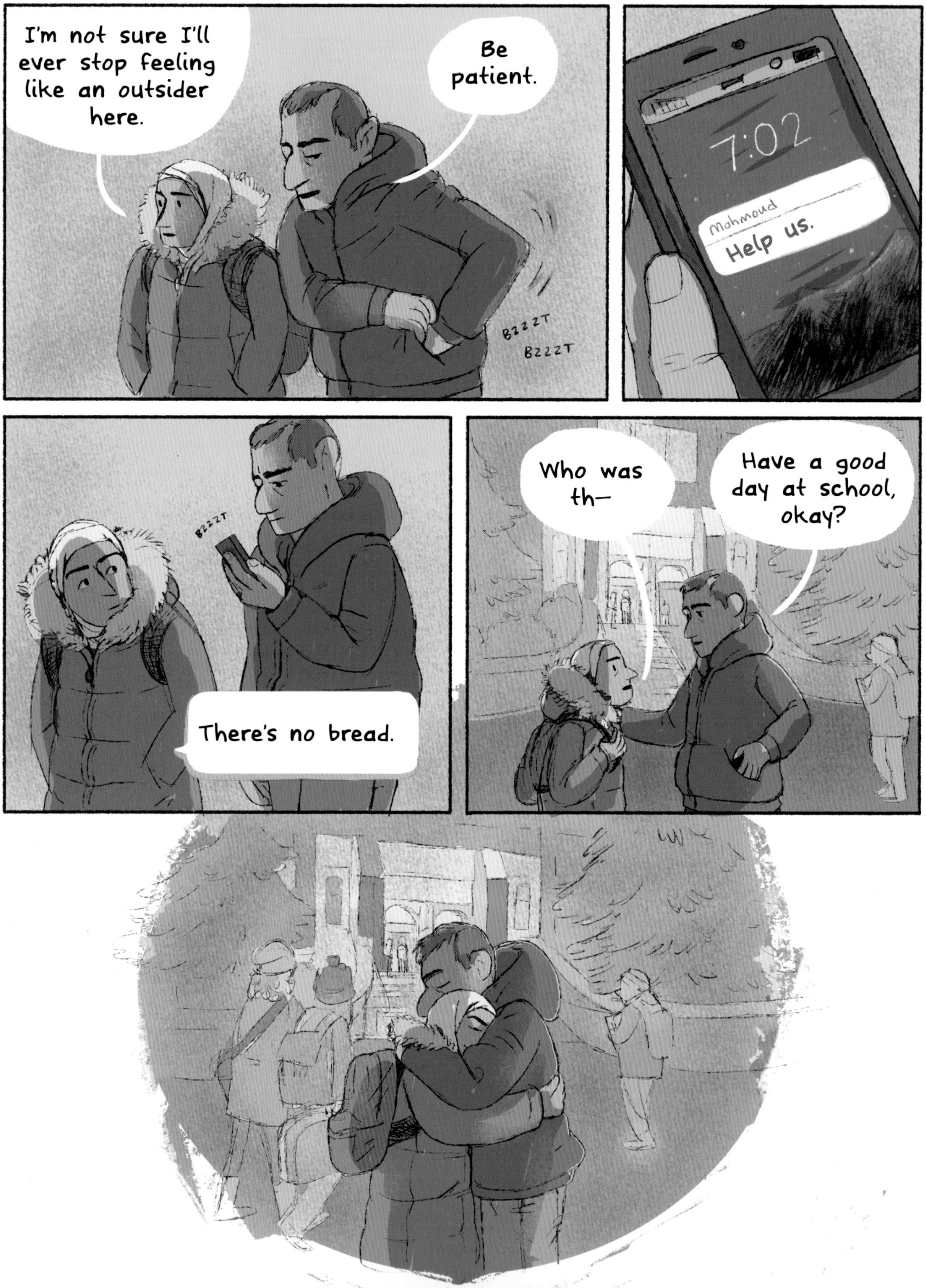
I'm not sure I'll ever stop feeling like an outsider here.
Be patient.
BZZZT
BZZZT
7:02
Mohmoud
Help us.
BZZZT
There's no bread.
Who was th–
Have a good day at school, okay?

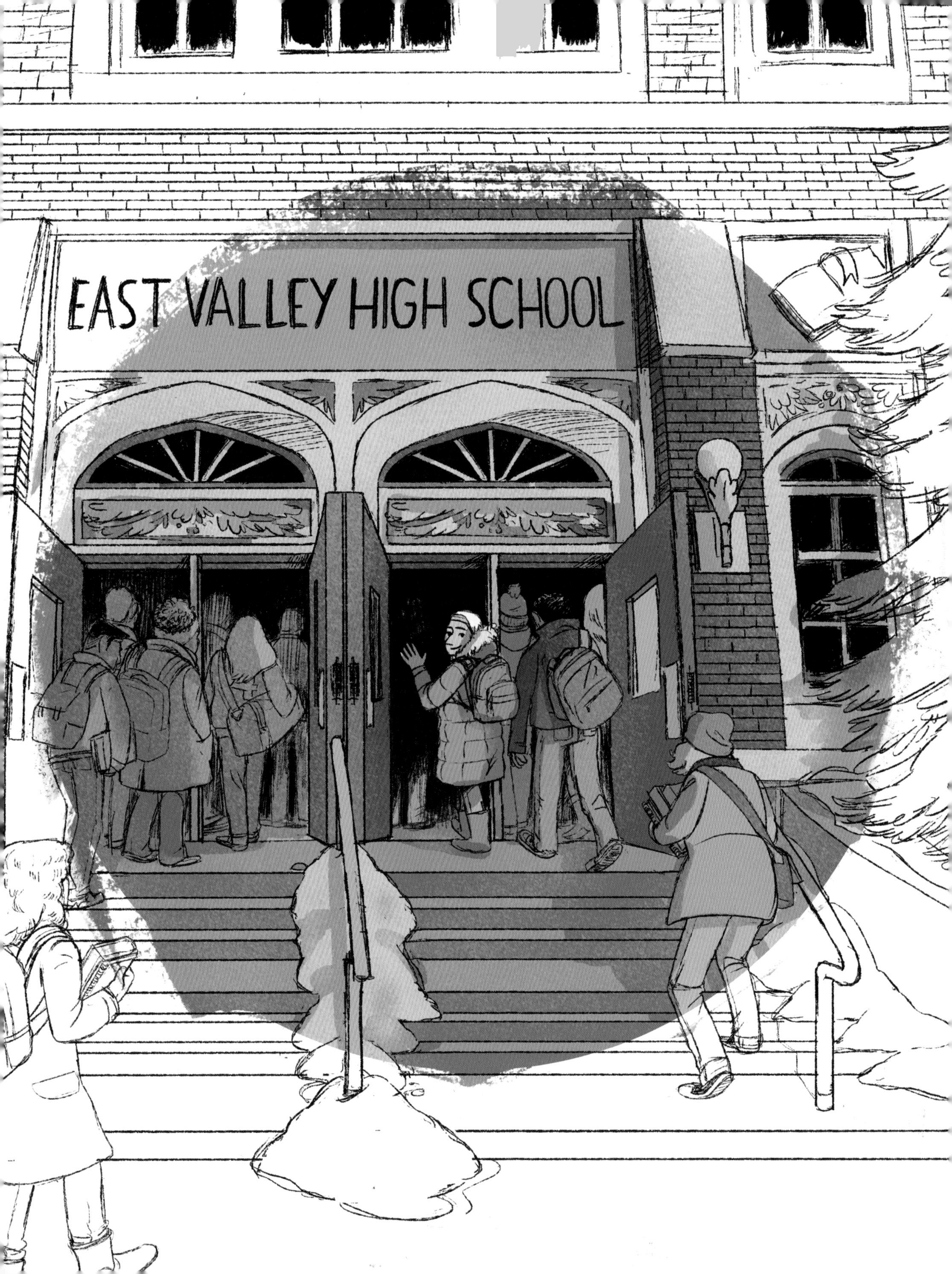
EAST VALLEY HIGH SCHOOL

Endnotes

It means war.

between civilian protestors and security forces at the Omari Mosque in Dara'a, and many analysts see this moment as a flash point in the early stages of the Syrian war. By 2017, three of the 15 boys were dead, and only half remained in Syria, according to reporting by the *Globe and Mail.*

- Between March and July 2011, mass protests to voice dissatisfaction with the authoritarian rule of Bashar al-Assad were met with brutality by police and government forces. Crackdowns on dissent and many arrests followed. Laws were changed to allow police — and the nation's 18 different security agencies — to detain civilians without warrant.

- April 2011, slogans had shifted from demanding government reform to overthrowing the Assad regime, and protests had spread to 20 cities. The Syrian army was deployed and initiated military attacks on protestors, leading to hundreds of civilian deaths.

- July 29, 2011, defecting Syrian army officers formed the Free Syria Army, which aimed to end Assad's hold on power. A coalition of Syrian opposition groups called the Syrian National Council was formed in Turkey on August 23. By September 2011, Syrian rebel forces, with active support from Turkey, launched an insurgency campaign across Syria.

- July 15, 2012, the International Committee of the Red Cross declared the fighting in Syria a civil war.

Syrians protest in Hama on July 29, 2011. Syrians took to the streets nationwide for the 17th consecutive Friday to demand an end to Bashar al-Assad's 11-year rule.

Page 12, "*Inshallah...*"

An Arabic word of Islamic origin, *inshallah* means "If God wills it" and is used widely in the Arab world to denote the speaker's hope of an event happening in the future.

Page 17, "It means war."

The uprising against Syrian president Bashar al-Assad turned into armed rebellion, and then civil war, after the following key events:

- On March 15, 2011, Activists call for a "Day of Rage" across Syria after the February arrest of 15 teenagers in the southern city of Dara'a who spray-painted a wall with the anti-government trademark of the Arab Spring: "The people want the fall of the regime." The students had been inspired by the use of the phrase in the revolutions in Cairo and Tunis. Their subsequent incarceration and torture lead to deadly confrontations

Page 18, "But the fight for Syria's freedom came at a violent price."

A UN fact-finding mission and a Commission of Inquiry both concluded that chemical weapons had been used by Syrian

But the fight for Syria's freedom came at a violent price.

pro-government forces in several attacks. The deadliest were in the Khal al-Assal suburbs of Aleppo in March 2013, in the Ghouta region of Damascus in August 2013 and in southern Idlib's Khan Sheikhoun on April 4, 2017. An eyewitness in Khan Sheikhoun reported to me shortly after the attack that victims had collapsed on the street and began frothing at the mouth — telltale signs of poisoning by a nerve agent. "They looked like they were drowning from the inside," he said. Several sources have determined the attacks likely used sarin gas, and the UN concluded the chemicals used came from the Syrian Army's stockpile. Death estimates are the largest in Ghouta and range widely from 250 to 1,700 people.

A man kneels among victims of a nerve gas attack carried out by the forces of Bashar al-Assad in the Ghouta region of Damascus, August 21, 2013.

Page 22, "When I leave, be sure I tried everything in my power to stay."

This powerful message was actually spray-painted on a wall in Homs, sometime after May 2014, and was first reported by rebel-friendly Homs Media Center.

Page 23, "Only six months?"

At the start of the crisis and until 2014, Lebanon did not change entry regulations for civilians fleeing embattled areas of Syria. New arrivals were given a six-month visa on arrival, renewable for another six months with payment

of a $200 fee. In light of the crisis, Lebanese authorities extended the time allotted to a full year — the cost remained $200. Syrians could renew their visa without charge, but to do so meant leaving the country for 24 hours. To save money, many refugees risked their lives to go back to Syria and reenter Lebanon. In 2015, new laws were introduced prohibiting this action — forcing Syrians to pay fees or risk becoming illegal residents.

Page 27, "Hajii Afaf says she will pay us 1,500 lira to sew these old shirts."

Lebanon's official currency is the Lebanese lira (L.L. or LBP), but U.S. dollars are also widely accepted. The lira is often used in smaller transactions, such as taxi fare and in convenience stores, but in high-end establishments and retail outlets, including pharmacies, the dollar is often quoted. Since December 1997 the rate of the Lebanese lira has been fixed at 1,500 L.L. per U.S. dollar.

Page 27, "It's not like the *mulukhiyah* at home, is it?"

Mulukhiyah is a popular Syrian dish made with stewed leaves of Nalta jute (also known as Jew's mallow).

Page 31, "... the UNHCR was billions of dollars short in humanitarian assistance."
The United Nations High Commissioner for Refugees (UNHCR) is the agency mandated to provide basic services to refugees, and the scale of its operations depends on what is admissible by the country in which it works. In Lebanon, the UNHCR is able to provide basic assistance, such as food and non-food aid, cash money, shelter and winter support. Due to funding shortfalls, the agency has had to scale back and refocus assistance to only the most vulnerable refugees. Top donors to the UNHCR according to funding reports for 2016 include the United States, Canada, Germany, the European Union, Norway and the United Kingdom.

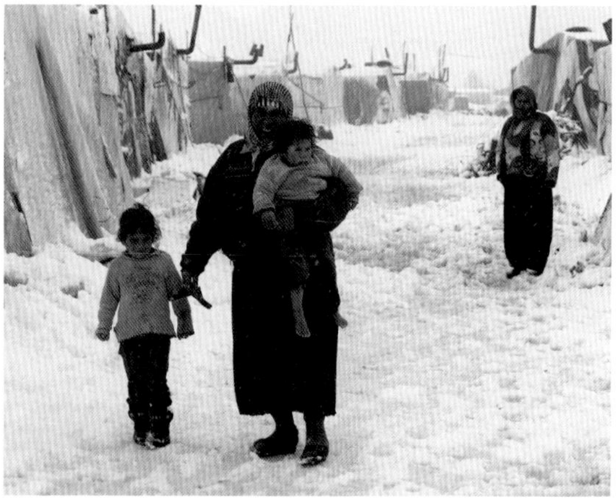

A Syrian refugee holds a barefoot child as she walks with a girl during a winter storm at a refugee camp in Zahle, in Lebanon's Bekaa Valley, January 7, 2015.

Page 31, "So instead of allowing Syrians to integrate into Lebanese society, they were kept separate."
Lebanon lacks a cogent policy for managing Syrian refugees, and efforts to devise such laws were hampered by sharp political and sectarian divides. The Future Movement, a party representing major Sunni-populated areas of Lebanon, appears to be more accommodating, but Christian parties such as the influential Free Patriotic Movement have firmly rejected calls to provide Syrian refugees with services and rights — formal camps and access to jobs, for example — that might encourage residency in Lebanon. Moreover, Lebanon has not signed the international convention that recognizes refugees, and therefore does not legally consider Syrians in its territories as such.

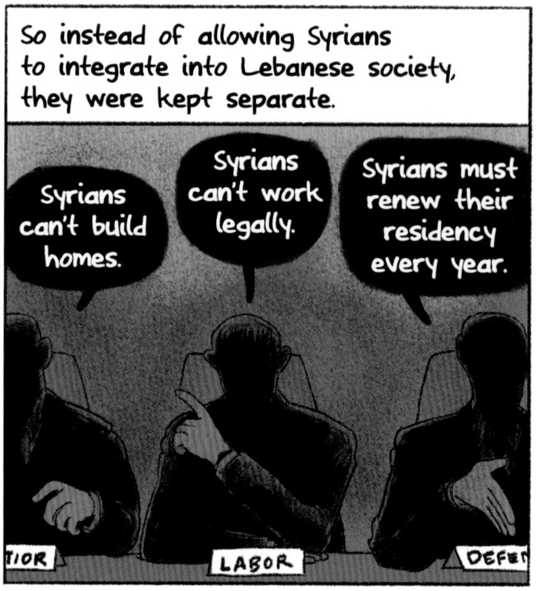
So instead of allowing Syrians to integrate into Lebanese society, they were kept separate.
Syrians can't build homes.
Syrians can't work legally.
Syrians must renew their residency every year.
LABOR

Page 33, "But I struggled to understand the curriculum, all in a language I had never seen."
Lebanon has a trilingual curriculum taught in English, French and Arabic. Syrian students enrolled in the formal school system face challenges following English and French components, having been taught only in Arabic in Syria. There are many similarities in Lebanese and Syrian dialects of Arabic, but it is not uncommon for the former to mix French and English into their daily speech. In one school in the Bekaa Valley, a teacher reported to me in 2013 that the Syrian refugee students in her class, confronted with the foreign language curriculum, had burst into tears.

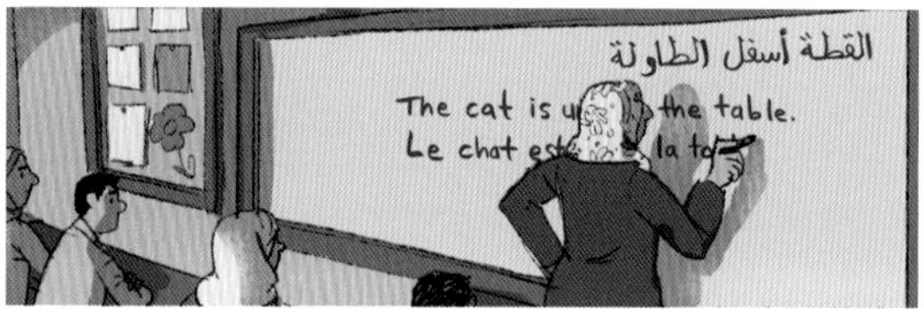
القطة أسفل الطاولة

Page 34, "*Wallah*, I don't know what to do."
Wallah is an Arabic saying meaning "I swear to God."

Page 38, "They had come to fight Hezbollah ..."
Hezbollah is an influential political party in Lebanon with a powerful paramilitary wing, whose fighters are active in Syria and Iraq. The party is backed financially and militarily by Iran and is currently led by Hasan Nasrallah. In Parliament, the party leads the March 8 coalition.

Page 42, "Okay, but don't make this a habit."

By 2015, many Syrian refugees were reporting to me that they were in deep debt — often to their grocers, pharmacists and landlords who deferred payment out of goodwill. I met Samira al-Homsi in Ansarieh, in Tyre, who owed the local pharmacist nearly $3,000 USD for medication she needed to manage her high blood pressure. "We don't make difficult decisions with our money, we make difficult sacrifices," she said.

Page 43, "Yes, I need you to take a break from school to help."

There are no reliable statistics to account for how many Syrian children are employed illegally in Lebanon, but an indication that the number is rising exponentially can be gauged through school attendance. Out of 480,000 school-aged Syrian children, only 33 percent are enrolled in school according to the International Labour Organization. Many Syrian child laborers work informally in agriculture for as little as $4 a day.

A Syrian refugee child works with his father sanding stone in the south of Sidon, southern Lebanon, April 30, 2014.

Page 45, "I will stop renewing my Lebanese residency papers."

According to UNHCR estimates in 2015, nearly 90 percent of registered refugees were trapped in debt. The average monthly income of a Syrian family then was $250 USD. To save on costs, most refugee families renewed residency visas for breadwinners only, which almost always meant the male head of the household. In our story, as the family's savings dwindled, Walid became the only member of the family to hold a valid visa. While Lebanese laws required that women and children have up-to-date papers, a security official explained to me that the authorities simply did not have the resources to track down all those who transgressed this rule. In 2015, Lebanon introduced new laws that required Syrians to not only pay $200 annually for legal residency but also find a Lebanese individual or company to sponsor their stay — a responsibility few Lebanese were willing to take. Those registered with the UNHCR were not required to find a sponsor but they were prohibited from working. By May 2015, the UNHCR stopped registering new arrivals, meaning all Syrians who entered the country after that time either did so illegally or paid the fee and found a sponsor. The new laws have led many refugees to live increasingly clandestine lives by avoiding checkpoints and rarely venturing outside camps.

Militant ISIS fighters take part in a military parade along the streets of Raqqa, Syria, after their declaration of an Islamic "caliphate," June 30, 2014.

Page 47, "Powerful Islamist and jihadist groups have emerged."

Abed's text messages coincide with the rising power and influence of the Islamic State in Iraq and Syria (ISIS) in the Syrian war. The group, formerly a splinter of Al-Qaeda, was founded in Iraq after the U.S. invasion of that country. ISIS expanded to Syria to exploit the chaos of civil war and gain leverage and land, declaring the city of Raqqa its capital in January 2014. Commanders of Free Syria Army battalions in the strategic region of Qalamoun, which borders Lebanon, reported to me in early 2015 that they were facing shortages in supplies, including food and arms, and many rebels were joining ISIS ranks.

A man walks through the wreckage following a barrel bomb air strike in Aleppo's district of al-Sukari, March 16, 2014.

Page 48, "Assad's sieges and starvation tactics have killed many."

The siege of Madaya in July 2015 is an extreme example of how the Bashar al-Assad regime successfully employed starvation tactics to force rebels to relinquish territory. By January 2016, horrific images emerged of emaciated children in Madaya, and individuals in the besieged city reported to me via WhatsApp that they were eating grass and domestic animals to survive.

Page 49, "I am afraid of what will happen to the 250,000 people trapped in eastern Aleppo."

The battle for Aleppo began in July 2012 and ran through the end of 2016, when the Syrian government agreed to evacuate rebel fighters and civilians living in the eastern district of the city to other opposition-held areas of the country. Tens of thousands were transported in buses and taken to Idlib, one of the last rebel-held provinces in Syria. During the siege, civilians living inside the eastern region of Aleppo reported to me that food supplies were always scarce and had dwindled to near nothing in December of 2016, before the evacuation. Several doctors reported they were running short on medicine, including painkillers, and were unable to treat the rising numbers of patients wounded by air strikes. According to monitors there were at least 23 recorded aerial attacks by the Assad regime and Russian forces on eastern Aleppo's eight hospitals.

Page 54, "Others were not."

The image of 3-year-old Alan Kurdi washed up ashore on a Turkish beach after he drowned in the Mediterranean Sea made global headlines in September 2015. He and his family were Syrian Kurdish refugees trying to reach Europe, after a failed attempt to seek asylum in Canada. The boy's death was felt disproportionately in Canada and was a key issue during the 2015 federal election. Then Liberal candidate Justin Trudeau vowed to bring 25,000 Syrian refugees to Canada as a major plank of the party's electoral platform.

Page 54, "It took us two weeks to cross five countries."

The refugee crisis in Europe began in 2015 when a rising number of people — many from Syria, but also from Afghanistan, Libya, Pakistan and Sudan — arrived illegally by boat in the European Union, traveling overland through southeast Europe to reach asylum in Germany and Sweden, mostly.

Page 55, "Yes, he says the Germans gave him a home and money."

The misconception that European governments would provide refugees with generous amounts of money and shelter was widespread among Syrians. Europe proved to be another struggle, and financial assistance given by a supporting state is barely enough to get by. In Germany, for example, one adult refugee gets €350 per month for basic needs, plus housing in specific areas. Similarly in Canada, one adult refugee living in the province of Ontario would receive, on average, $768 CAD monthly for basic needs, plus a one-time start-up allotment of roughly $2,065 CAD. Refugees in Canada are also provided housing, but must take over the cost of rent once they are settled. The maximum amount government-assisted refugee families are given in Canada is $25,000 CAD in the year they arrive (this includes the monthly amounts and start-up allotment).

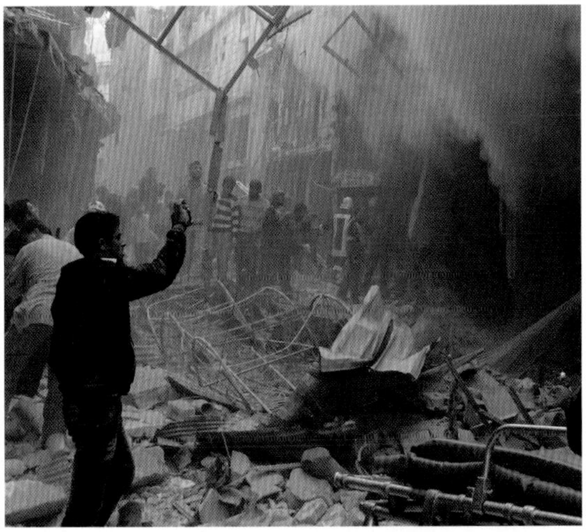

Residents inspect a site damaged by explosive barrels dropped by forces loyal to Syria's president Bashar Al-Assad in the Al-Shaar neighborhood of Aleppo, April 6, 2014.

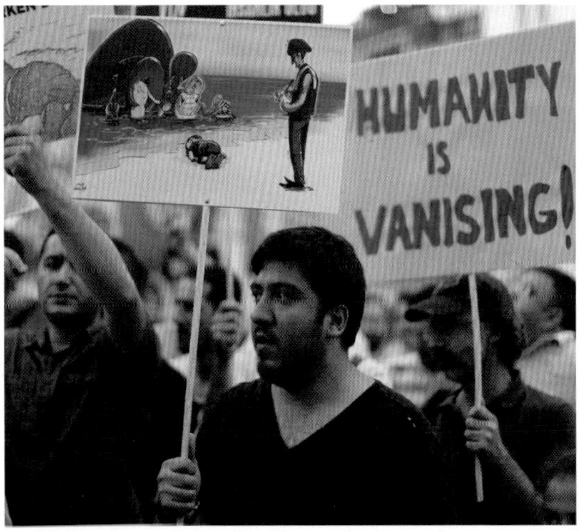
HUMANITY
IS
VANISING!

Turkish protestors hold signs depicting drowned Syrian toddler Alan Kurdi during a demonstration for refugee rights in Istanbul, September 3, 2015.

Page 57, Lebanon/Europe Pros and Cons
When I met the al-Arda family in July 2015 in Shatila camp, the family was considering joining several other refugees who were paying smugglers to take them to Turkey from Tripoli port and onward to Europe from there. Inspired by a journalist colleague who had done the same, I suggested they make a pro-and-con list. When I met them again a few months later in November, Mohamed Arda, the father, had made it to Germany and his wife Najwa was diligently making the $200 monthly payments to their creditor, a Lebanese neighbor who had taken out a loan for them in his name. "We will go to Germany too, when the papers come through," she had said then. When I last heard from them in December 2016, she and her three children were still waiting.

Page 58, "Do you understand the terms?"
Unable to secure bank loans, refugees with limited financial means and a desire to attempt a sea crossing had no choice but to sell their belongings, beg Lebanese friends to take out loans for them or ask loan sharks for money to pay boat smugglers. In this deal Walid accepts a loan of $5,000 USD from Abu Haidar with an interest rate of 10 percent and payments due monthly.

Page 64, "The smugglers are monsters."
Turkey-bound smuggling activity peaks in the summer. An intelligence officer told me in August 2015 that those caught were disproportionately Syrian and Palestinian refugees whose visas had expired. Smugglers typically demand $1,500-$2,000 per passenger, and in several instances refugees found out they had been deceived after doling out the money. Those who had second thoughts were often forced onto already crammed boats, and the use of fake life jackets was reported widely by refugees who had reached Turkey.

Page 70, "We're preparing for a siege."
In 2016, Bashar al-Assad's forces, with the help of Russian air strikes, closed the last remaining supply line into the rebel-held eastern district of Aleppo and set about a siege to recapture the territory. Air strikes used barrel bombs, bunker-buster bombs and phosphorous bombs to target civilian residences and medical facilities.

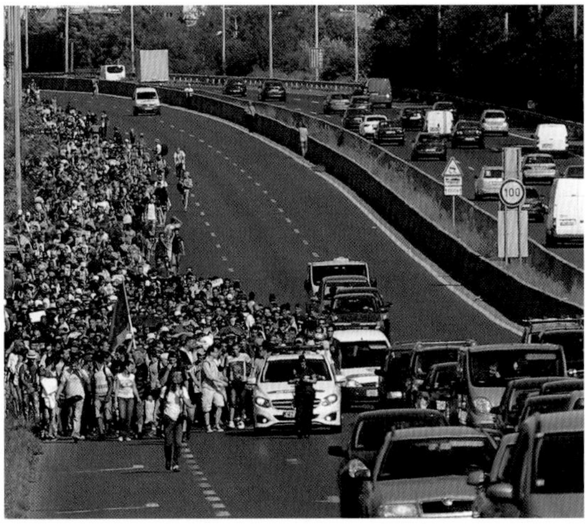

Migrants march along the highway out of Budapest, Hungary, and toward the Austrian border, September 4, 2015.

The Syria Civil Defense, also known as the White Helmets — a volunteer organization operating in rebel-held parts of Syria — came to prominence in the West during news coverage of the siege. The group had emerged in 2012 and now consists of several dozen teams with more than 3,000 members.

In September 2016, I spoke to Beebers Mishal, a member of the White Helmets in Aleppo during the worst aerial onslaught before the district fell under regime control in December of that year. He described how units dashed to the scene of an aerial attack moments after hearing the explosion and often had to dig for hours to pull civilians from the rubble. "After one attack, an 11-day-old baby was missing. We found her by listening to the sound of her crying from beneath the wreckage," he said.

Members of the White Helmets rescue children after barrel bombs were dropped in the al-Shaar neighborhood of Aleppo, June 2, 2014.

Page 72, "I've come to invite you to my wedding."

According to a study by St. Joseph University in Lebanon, 23 percent of female Syrian refugees were child brides. Ramona Idriss, a psychologist working for Himaya, an NGO providing psychosocial support to Syrian refugees in the Bekaa Valley, said she was following at least 50 such cases, some involving child brides as young as 9. These girls often suffered severe physical and mental trauma after the wedding night and suffered a host of health complications after childbirth. Child marriage existed in Syria before the conflict, but the onset of war caused rates to rise dramatically. Some parents had told Idriss that they were marrying off their daughters to protect them from sexual harassment in camps.

Page 77, "We think your family would make a good candidate for resettlement."

Resettlement is a multilayered process. Refugees cannot nominate themselves, and have to be recommended by UN workers. Those selected for consideration by the UN resettlement unit are first asked whether they are willing to participate, then they are interviewed several times. Resettlement countries also have their own individual criteria and it is up to the UN to match family and country. Once cases are submitted, embassies carry out their own line of interviews and background checks and acquire biometric data. The process can take anywhere from a few months to several years, as it does for Syrians being resettled to the United States, for example.

Page 79, "To go to Syria, my mother had to prepare."

As unusual as it might appear, buses will take Syrians to ISIS-held areas of Syria from Lebanon for a fee of $50 USD

I've come to invite you to my wedding.

each way. Abu Hamad, a bus driver, told me the journey to Raqqa could span between 20 hours and three days depending on the fighting. Most passengers are typically workers going to visit their families. The strict interpretations of Islamic law have men planning in advance to grow out a beard before the journey and women making sure to pack black abayas.

Page 81, "For smuggling in cigarettes you will be punished ..."

Life under ISIS rule is brutal because of the group's strict policies. Smoking cigarettes and listening to music are outlawed, and public punishments take place routinely. Women rarely venture out for fear of being reprimanded by the ISIS police.

Page 82, "We were told we would be welcomed, like those who arrived before us."

Refugees coming to Canada fall under three categories: They can be privately sponsored by a group of five or more Canadians; they can be government-assisted refugees; or they can be part of a scheme that mixes the two called the Blended Visa-Office Referred (BVOR) program, in which refugees receive financial assistance from sponsors and the government. Government-assisted refugees receive social assistance and support from a caseworker but not the social network that comes with private sponsorship, which has proven to be a key factor in refugee integration. Of all the Syrian refugees resettled in Canada, the majority, approximately 21,800, are government-assisted while 14,000 are privately sponsored. Just under 4,000 are in the BVOR category. According to the Government of Canada, 40,000 Syrian refugees had resettled in the country as of January 2017.

Acknowledgments

I wish to thank my editors at the *Daily Star* and the *Globe and Mail*, Mirella Hodeib and Susan Sachs, for their mentorship and trust, which allowed me to report deeply on the refugee crisis in Lebanon.

To my partner in crime, the endlessly talented Jackie Roche, for bringing this story to life and guiding me through the subtle arts of comic-book writing — I am honored to share authorship with you. I am eternally grateful to our wonderful and tireless editor, Steve Cameron, for first, conceiving of this project, and second, engaging me to write it. I could not have dreamed of a better team than the two of you to spend hours poring over scripts with.

For veering me away from the rookie mistakes of comic scripting — in under an hour — I thank Ty Templeton. For their constant love and support, I am grateful to my parents and my partner, Stephen Kalin. Most importantly, I thank the countless Syrian refugees who, even in the midst of extreme privation, welcomed me into their homes and entrusted me with their stories.

— S.K.

Thank you to Steve Cameron, editorial director at Firefly Books, for initiating this project and for his enthusiasm, insightful edits and patience. Thank you and much respect to Samya Kullab for her reporting work and for her bold sprint into the comics medium. It was an honor to draw this book. Thanks also to Mike Freiheit for jumping in as colorist and for his hard work bringing life to my drawings, and to Firefly Books for bringing this book to young readers.

— J.R.